SEA RED,
SEA BLUE

Jean James &
Mary James

GW00802559

Contact Information: titleadmin@pelicanbookgroup.com

Scripture quotations, unless otherwise indicated are taken from the King James translation, public domain.

Cover Art by *Nicola Martinez*

Harbourlight Books, a division of Pelican Ventures, LLC
www.pelicanbookgroup.com PO Box 1738 *Aztec, NM * 87410

Harbourlight Books sail and mast logo is a trademark of Pelican Ventures, LLC

Publishing History
First Harbourlight Edition, 2014
Paperback Edition ISBN 978-1-61116-327-8
Electronic Edition ISBN 978-1-61116-326-1
Published in the United States of America

Dedication

To our loving and supportive families

1

The sound of screeching brakes drew Katherine to her frosted apartment window. Evidently, a late blizzard intended to swoop down on Chicago. After one glance at the icy roads, she decided to walk the six blocks to the church social. Probably few church members would brave the weather, but she needed some diversion to scour the residue of a horrible day from her mind.

Two minutes of the outside chill convinced Katherine she should have remained in her warm apartment. The almost deserted streets and empty sidewalks looked incredibly lonesome for that usually bustling neighborhood. Big flakes of snow rushed to bury the ice-covered walk, muting her footsteps. A few scattered streetlamps did their best to look friendly, but the snow dulled even their company. When wind penetrated brazenly through her usually adequate winter clothes, she pulled her collar up and quickened her pace.

A series of shrill horn blasts from somewhere behind startled her. She turned in time to see a speeding black car dash in front of a silver SUV. The SUV slid to a halt barely in time to avoid a collision. The vehicle's driver blasted noisy, but vain rebukes while the offending car leaped from the road and shot across a parking lot straight at Katherine.

As the car came closer, a shaft of light from a street

lamp revealed the outline of a large man hunched over the steering wheel.

Katherine sprang towards a pile of snow and realized, even as she dove, that she was too late. Just as the car reached her, the tires hit a patch of ice, and the vehicle began a crazy circular spin. When the car came out of the spin, it slid sideways almost thirty feet across the lot. Something brushed against her, knocked her purse to the ground and smacked her arm.

The motorist in the SUV eased up on the horn and drove closer to the curb to witness the catastrophe sure to befall the maniac driver, but the man had regained control of his car. He circled the lot and headed back in the direction he had come from, still at break-neck speed.

Katherine rose from the slushy pile of snow hardly able to believe she had escaped.

The SUV's driver rolled down her window. "Are you all right?" she shouted. Not waiting for an answer, she rolled her window back up to block out the wind and snow.

Katherine waved her hand. "I'm OK." Her voice sounded strange and inadequate, but the driver evidently understood her message and drove away.

For a minute, Katherine remained too stunned to think. She tried to tell herself it was an accident, but some part of her *knew* that the driver had his car under perfect control when he turned towards her, *knew* that an ice patch had saved her life.

She stood there in the temporarily deserted night, and a shiver, not caused by the cold, passed over her body. She scooped up her snow-filled purse and started to run back to the warmth and safety of her apartment, but her legs shook out of control, and she took a nasty fall. With a twisted ankle and a jammed wrist, she started again at a fast limp, but even after she had locked her apartment door and pulled shut all the curtains, her heart still thudded heavily.

With lights off, she sat on the sofa by the front window and peeked around the curtain at the dark street. Repeatedly she revisualized the outline of the driver as he bore down on her—his large shape hugging the steering wheel. She couldn't subdue her mind's imagination or speculation. Had she suffered an impulsive act by some deranged thrill seeker or a premeditated act? Was the driver someone who knew her—a stalker or someone with a grudge?

She shivered and continued to examine each passing car. Once she thought she recognized a black car that cruised slowly by—too slowly. When the same car crept by a second time and slowed almost to a stop as it drew even with her apartment, her heart jolted. The vehicle looked like the car that had bumped her, black, shiny, and sporty, but she didn't know car models that well.

She kneeled on the sofa with her face pressed to the window and her cell phone in her hand. If the car came by again, she would not only call the police, she would take a picture of the offending vehicle with her phone camera. An hour passed and the car didn't show. She pulled the curtain shut, too tired to continue her vigil. Though still chilled, the worst of her panic had abated. She went for a blanket and turned up the thermostat.

Leaning back against a sofa pillow with her knees pulled up and the blanket wrapped around her, she gazed around the dark, familiar room. She wanted to settle her mind on something besides the man in the black car, something happier and less scary, but the cheerless room didn't help. Maybe she shouldn't renew her lease. Her forty-five-day renewal notice came that day, and they had raised her rent again. She could afford a better apartment in a better location if she stayed with her real estate job, but that thought troubled her, too.

Katherine asked herself for the hundredth time why she went into sales work when she didn't enjoy sales. At length, she realized that the evening's fright had amplified her discontent in every area. She wished she knew what to do about it.

In the intense quietness of the room, she longed for a friendly voice. She reached for her phone, ready to call her mother, but quickly put it down. The car incident would frighten her mom, and if she brought up the subject of her restlessness, it would only renew an old quarrel. She knew how her mother felt about her "wonderful career opportunity." Yet Mother lived the life she wanted to live in New York City and didn't apologize to anyone for her choice.

All at once, Katherine missed her father and wished he was still alive to advise her. He would understand. She stared over at her favorite picture, a blown-up snapshot of her dad and her on a rental motorboat. It was a prized memento of a long-ago Florida vacation. That glorious day had been her father's gift for her twelfth birthday. The two of them had spent the day on the Atlantic, glorying in the ocean. Though she couldn't see the picture clearly in the dimly lit room, every detail stood out clearly in her mind.

The spell of the sea filled their eyes and radiated from their burnt, smiling faces. A month later, her father had died, and though Florida gleamed in her memory like an earthly paradise, she hadn't been near the ocean since. She walked over and took the picture down. When she returned to the sofa, she snuggled it close to her under the blanket. Lying there in the darkness, she prayed silently, *I know You must have something more planned for me, Lord. Please show me my path.*

****

The ring of her phone startled her awake from restless, dream filled sleep. Morning had arrived too quickly and with it had come a jolting flashback of her incident with the wild driver. She hurried to answer the call.

"H-Hello."

"Good morning, Katherine. Hope I didn't wake you. I just had a call from the bank. Their vice president, Mr. Pinkston, said you'd left a folder there yesterday."

"Yes, I did. Thank you, Lloyd. The bank closed before I realized I had left it. I'll pick it up as soon as they open."

An extended, uncomfortable silence followed and she wondered if he had heard her.

"I...will you...be coming by the office today?" he finally asked.

"Right after I run by the bank."

"Good. I'll see you, then."

That was strange. Why would the bank call her broker, and why would Lloyd call at seven fifteen in the morning over something so trivial? He never called before ten. *I guess last night's scare is causing me to question everything.*

"Maybe it *was* an accident," she said aloud, "a crazy accident."

Daylight had relieved some of her trepidation, but the face that stared from the mirror seemed paler than usual and the green eyes expressed genuine agitation. Those eyes told her to believe what she wanted, *they* knew what they had seen, and when she looked deep into them, she saw more than fright. Real longing for a new chance at life blazed out from behind the fear and said, "Be bold. Don't wait."

When she left an hour later, her anxiety began to build again. She searched for lurking black cars and constantly checked her rearview mirror. Just as she pulled into the bank's parking lot, she saw Lloyd's car leave. He must have had business there, too. She hoped her business would only entail picking up the folder. She didn't want to face Mr. Pinkston, who had dismissed her like a naughty child when she questioned the insurance claim. Maybe he hadn't arrived yet. She hurried in and straight over to the secretary's desk.

"I left a folder in Mr. Pinkston's office yesterday."

"Please go right in. He'll see you shortly."

She groaned inwardly. Must she confront the man again? She took a deep breath and went through the door into his empty office. The folder's contents held no great importance to her because she had made copies of most of the papers in it, but it did contain the letter she meant to publicize if the bank didn't honor their agreement. She hadn't wanted them to see that unless she was forced to use it.

Fifteen minutes later the secretary came through the door with the folder. Evidently, Pinkston didn't want to see her any more than she wanted to see him. Self-consciousness prevailed when she left his office. It seemed like the entire bank knew of the matter, but no one looked her way except one man who waited in a chair outside Pinkston's office. When he continued his intense scrutiny, her discomfiture turned into paranoia. She needed to go outside where the cold wind would blow away her foolishness—where tiny incidents wouldn't unnerve her. She avoided the man's eyes when she passed him, but he followed her out the front door of the bank.

"Ma'am...excuse me, Ma'am."

A southern accent tinged his low, mellow voice—a friendly voice. She turned around.

"I'm trying to locate someone. It's extremely important I find this person. He might work at the bank here, or...he could be a friend or associate of Mr. Pinkston. His name..."

"I don't work here. I'm a *customer*." She hadn't meant to snap in such a hostile tone, but the name jabbed into her already raw nerves.

He winced and his hazel eyes flashed a look of surprise.

"Excuse me," she said in a kinder tone.

He looked cold. The wind blew his dark-brown hair straight out. He wasn't dressed for early spring in Chicago. His thin, gray suit set off his tan, though. It looked like real suntan, a Florida tan.

"Have you tried his secretary? She might know something."

His amused expression flustered her. Had she been staring at him while he waited for her to speak? She certainly wasn't acting like herself today.

"My apologies, Ma'am. You came from his office,

and I took it for granted *you* were his secretary." He didn't wait for her reply, but hurried off down the sidewalk.

This looked to be the start of another awful day.

2

She made her way through traffic and dirty, snow lined streets to the real estate office. While she stomped slush from her shoes, the office door obligingly opened.

"Thank you, Lloyd," she said to the tall man who hurried her into the office. In spite of her haste, a blast of chilly air followed her in. "Business must be downright slow if my broker works the door."

"Nice day, isn't it? Such a cold, miserable, gray, windy Chicago day."

"I wonder what it's like in Florida right now."

"About eighty degrees with sunshine, probably." He smiled and glanced out the window.

"What a terrible thing to tell someone who dreams every night of palm trees and beaches and a blue-green ocean."

Lloyd laughed. "You and your talk of Florida. Let me know when you plan to leave. We'll put together a luau to send you off."

Everyone had heard her threats to leave Chicago and move to the land of sunshine.

"Not this week, anyway," she said as she removed her coat. "I have to deal with tiresome bank trouble over a friend's insurance claim. With all the business our office gives them, you'd think we could expect civility."

"Come into my office and tell me about it. Maybe I

can help."

Surprised at his offer, she followed him in. Although Lloyd could be friendly, even joke on occasion, he rarely got involved with his associate's problems unless they involved a real estate deal about to be consummated—or lost.

"What's the trouble?" he asked as he closed the door and settled at his desk.

"You remember when I sold that two-story affair on Burton Street to my friend Laura and her husband? The Frasers?" She rummaged in her briefcase for copies of the papers she had given to the bank.

"The Abbott house, you mean? Nice home."

"Not now. Those storms we had a couple of weeks ago caused a lot of damage. The Frasers have an arrangement where they pay their insurance premium directly to the bank, but now the bank claims there's no such agreement. These papers prove otherwise." She handed the two documents to him.

"Mr. Pinkston has seen these?" He asked as he skimmed the papers.

"I left copies with him yesterday, and I threatened to give this information to the newspaper and the consumer helps reporter on Channel 4 if the bank didn't take care of this matter by Friday."

A frown tightened Lloyd's face. He bowed his gray head over the papers and studied them more closely. When he returned his attention to Katherine, his smile and easy-going manner had returned. "Don't go any further with this until I see what I can accomplish."

"Thank you. Actually, I didn't plan any more action...until Friday, anyway." Before she left, she added, "I have more copies of those papers, so I won't need them back. I'll be at my desk off and on today if you need me."

Katherine filled her coffee cup and set it down by the disordered pile of documents on her desk. Too unsettled to pursue sales leads, she decided to organize upcoming work. An hour later, she had two neat piles of papers and an empty coffee cup. One pile contained leads and sales opportunities. The other pile was sales that awaited consummation—three closings due to come up in the next few weeks.

She decided she needed a break and walked down the block to a donut shop. After ordering a large espresso and a cream filled donut, she tried to relax, but every black car in the passing traffic caught her attention. Another fear filled night loomed.

Her cell phone beeped with a call from Lloyd. Expecting news about Laura's house, she greeted him with some degree of apprehension.

"Katherine, you can relax about the Frasers' problem. I have influence with the board of directors at that bank, and I've put someone to work on it there."

"You can't imagine what it will mean to the Frasers if something can be done."

"Actually, the Frasers are meeting with Mr. Pinkston right now." The pleased tone of his voice said more than his words.

"That's the best news I've had all year. Thank you, Lloyd. I'll be back in the office shortly." Katherine picked up her untouched donut and enjoyed it.

Five minutes later a bubbling-over Laura called. "They've taken care of everything, Kay. Not only will they pay our rent while they repair our house, but the settlement will be more than we expected."

"Did they explain why they suddenly changed

their minds?"

"Oh…yes. They said that a new employee hadn't paid the premium. He didn't know that the bank held part of our payment money in escrow for insurance, and he filed the papers away in the wrong place, so no one caught the mistake. Anyway, they fired him, and everything's OK now. Thank you for all that you did."

"I'm glad, Laura."

Laura went into a lengthy description of her rebuilding plans. She literally overflowed with ideas for her old-new castle.

"Have they put everything in writing for you?" Katherine asked when Laura stopped for a breath.

"They're getting the papers ready. I guaranteed them we wouldn't pursue any publicity, or anything of that sort. I don't want to anger them now that they're so generous." She giggled happily. "Kay, I'll call you back. We have to go in now."

Relief flooded Katherine. She hadn't expected such swift results. She swallowed the rest of her coffee and headed back to the office.

When Lloyd saw her, he motioned her into his office. "Come in, Katherine. Close the door, would you, and have a seat."

"Thank you so much for your help with the Frasers. Laura is ecstatic." She settled into a plush leather chair.

"I'm glad that concern won't trouble you anymore."

"Yes, but it does bother me the way the bank acted almost…deceitful. Maybe something more should be done."

"An honest mistake, I'm sure. I'd forget it, Katherine. By the way, the bank faxed me a statement that admits their liability in this matter. It guarantees they will honor Frasers' claim promptly and with additional compensation for the delay and mix-up. I made you a copy to use in case you've already contacted any news media and need to show them something official to cancel pending actions." He handed her the sheet of paper.

She examined the brief, three-sentence statement. Mr. Pinkston admitted the bank's liability, listed the name of the employee who made the error, and signed it at the bottom. "I'll file it away with my other papers, but I won't need to use it. I haven't contacted any media, yet. Thanks to you, that won't be necessary."

He gave her his best salesman's smile. "Now, I have an idea that might appeal to you. Your mention of Florida this morning made me think of it. You've made it clear for some time that you're contemplating a move there, and this morning I happened to get a call from a broker friend of mine who lives in Naples, Florida. That's a spot you'd really love, right on the Gulf, white-sand beaches, wonderful climate. He has new condominium projects that have just reached the sales stage, and he needs salespeople to sell the units."

Katherine had mentioned Florida many times, had even threatened to move there, but no one had taken her seriously—or had they? "Naples sounds like a wonderful place, but I'm not licensed to sell in Florida."

"You wouldn't need a license with him. He owns quite a few condominium complexes and office buildings. You could sell directly for him until you have a chance to take the Florida real estate course and get your license."

"That sounds like a very pleasant prospect, but…"

"Let me check further into it. By the way, what deals do you have pending?"

"Three closings, all of them should come up this month."

"It would be a shame to let them get in the way of an opportunity like this. I could easily handle the closings and mail your commission checks to you. Listen, I have to talk with him again in a little while. Let me get all the particulars on this for you."

"Thank you." She nodded, uncertain. "I have to run home for a while." When she rose to leave his office, he came over and shook her hand.

"I'm glad I can help a little in this matter, too. I know how you feel about Florida."

He might as well have fired me, she thought ruefully as she drove homeward. *Brokers aren't supposed to act like that when they are about to lose one of their top salespeople.*

When she pulled into her parking space, her side mirror revealed a black car parked along the adjacent road—the vehicle resembled last night's car. The man in the driver's seat gazed in her direction. Before she could take a closer look, the car melted into the traffic.

Her hands shook so violently she could hardly unlock her apartment door. After a quick study of the street, she pulled the door closed. Although it felt foolish, she searched the closet and under the bed.

Katherine turned her thoughts to the life-changing decision that lay before her. She had come home to consider Lloyd's Florida idea, unhampered by his influence or counsel. She picked up the picture of her father and stared into his loving eyes, as if he could advise her in the dilemma. The sudden ring of her phone startled her and she fumbled the photo to answer the call.

"Katherine, good news—*great* news, for you!" Lloyd answered her timid hello. "I talked again with that broker I told you about, Buzzy Amano. He said you could start work immediately. In fact, it's imperative that you go at once, because he has to put someone in that job right away. I'd recommend leaving tomorrow since you have a twenty-hour drive ahead of you. The job involves both sales and office work, and he'll pay wages until you get your real estate license. He also said he'd help you find an apartment when you get there. Now how does that sound?"

She had heard Lloyd use that master-salesman's voice before. At least, he couldn't see her face as she stood there speechless, her over-whelmed mind trying to process his information.

"Katherine? Are you there?"

"OK. I guess I could leave tomorrow. That sounds…fine." Katherine wondered if the lure of Florida was clouding her judgement, but last night's episode intruded on those thoughts.

"Good girl. I need you to organize your closing papers, and we'll go over them at the office later today. Goodbye, until then."

This is crazy! I'm crazy. Her peaceful life now marched to a fast double time, and she could barely catch her breath. Lloyd's call may have brought the matter to a head, but she knew he hadn't caused her decision. The black car had already triggered an alarm inside her. She was afraid to stay in Chicago.

"I'd better pack now, before I weaken," she told the picture she still held in her hand. Her father seemed to smile his approval and blessing. "And I'll pack you, first."

She gently wrapped the picture in a robe and placed it in a suitcase before she went on to survey the rest of the apartment. At least she had rented it furnished. Her few personal belongings would fit easily into her car.

After she called the apartment manager, she plunged into the task with an energy she hadn't felt for a long time. The outside temperature didn't encourage fussiness, so the job went fast. She bestowed the overflow on a shocked, but grateful next-door neighbor, and far sooner than expected, she emptied her apartment of everything except a pillow, some blankets, and an overnight bag.

Late that afternoon, Katherine returned to her office and found Lloyd ready for her. It didn't take long to review the pending closings. Just as they completed their business, one of Lloyd's clients arrived for a conference. With no time for further talk, he handed her the phone number and address of the Naples realtor.

"Good luck, Katherine. We'll miss you. By the way, your new broker likes to be called Big Buzzy."

With Lloyd ensconced behind closed doors, and the only other associate in the office busy with a young couple, there would be no sad good-byes. She cleaned out her desk, bade the room a silent farewell, and left.

"I'll send you postcards from Florida," Katherine shouted to the ice streaked windows of the real estate office as she drove away.

Dead tired when she got back to the empty apartment, she looked around. No good night's sleep awaited, not with the memory of the car incident to unnerve her. The descending darkness magnified everything. She couldn't spend another night.

She stuffed the last few items into the car, dropped off her apartment key and a final month's rent check, and drove away. She gripped the steering wheel with nervous hands and watched for the black car.

Katherine had hardly gone three miles when, all at once, everything felt very right. She laughed as she toiled through work traffic—her *last* Chicago work traffic. Though physically weary, her exhilaration chased away drowsiness. Sooner than expected, she reached her first goal, Interstate 65—*south*.

"It will grow warmer every mile," she announced to the face in the mirror.

No fear clouded the eyes that sparkled back now. Her whole face glowed with excitement. She set her cruise control and eagerly watched the mile markers count up her progress. An enchanted highway stretched out ahead, and she was determined to drive at least five-hundred miles closer to her dream before daylight.

3

Two days later, with open car windows and her hair blowing in the warm breeze, Katherine reached Naples. Her front seat held an assortment of tourist cravings, including oranges, grapefruit, a log of pecan divinity, and a dozen postcards. Her left arm had turned pink with sunburn from resting on the windowsill, and she wore shorts, a halter-top, and a happy smile.

"Could you please tell me how far I am from the beach—I mean a place where I can park my car and walk out on the beach?" she asked at a service station in town.

The attendant grinned in understanding. He took out a sheet of paper and drew a simple map. "These avenues all end at the beach, and there's parking at them. This one ends at the city fishing pier, and you can get to the beach there, too."

She thanked him and followed the map straight to the Gulf. When she pulled into a parking space at the end of one of the avenues, a delightful view of sand and water greeted her. She took in the grandeur of the scene, but she hadn't come to sit and look. She locked the car and walked out onto the glistening white beach.

Thank You, God, for this! Thank you for bringing me safely here, she prayed as she watched the sun set. Water rolled up and seagulls dipped into foamy waves. It was better than she had expected. *Thank You for giving me the courage to come.*

She wondered if anyone could have such a grand feeling upon arrival in Chicago, and then she laughed. Of course, they could. Chicago would suit some people. But this suited her.

For half an hour, she walked the water's edge, her shoes left behind. Finally, she pulled away and found lodging at a small, family owned motel—an older place almost buried in tropical vegetation and mature fruit trees.

"There's plenty of ripe fruit on the trees behind the rooms—oranges and carambolas, and I don't know what all else you might find. Just help yourself," the jolly, gregarious owner told her.

Katherine tramped all over the motel grounds to see the flowers and trees. She loved everything about Naples, especially the friendly, informal manner of the people.

Daybreak found her at the same parking space she had used the evening before. With one full day to play tourist before she had to report for work, she threw sandals into the car and ran down to the water's edge. Although she wore a swimsuit, the chilly surf that swirled around her ankles didn't encourage swimming. A scan of the distant beach revealed a few other early risers, but only one dared the cold water.

The hard, wet sand felt good to her feet as she started on a long walk. Presently, a boat on the horizon drew her attention. *How picturesque.*

She would take a boat out on the beautiful Gulf in memory of her father and their day on the ocean. Maybe God would let him peek down from heaven and enjoy it with her. She watched the boat's progress until a long pier broke her line of sight, probably the fishing pier the station attendant had mentioned. When she reached its rough wooden stairs, she climbed eagerly to the planks above.

Most of the people there were fishing. After she had walked the pier's length, she rested on one of the wooden benches by the rail. The clear water revealed schools of fish in its depths. Boats of all sizes passed at a safe distance from the fishing lines, and she studied them with intense interest. It felt grand to sit there, breathe in the salt air, and listen to the water and the birds.

After a while, a young boy and girl changed their fishing location to a spot close by. Lying flat on their stomachs at the pier's edge, they fished around the pilings below.

"Have you caught anything?" Katherine asked.

"I got this sheepshead," the little girl said proudly and jumped up to exhibit a good sized, black-banded fish in a plastic bucket.

"What did you use for bait?"

"Shrimp. A teeny piece of shrimp."

"Do you catch other kinds of fish here?"

"Snapper and angelfish and—"

"And pinfish and cats," the boy said. "But snapper and sheepshead are the best eatin' fish." They showed her their tackle, and she studied how their rods were rigged. Soon they announced they had to go home for lunch.

Katherine bought a drink and snacks at the pier's shop and continued her leisurely beach walk. Midday she left the beach and took a self-guided tour of Naples, assuming that her job might require some knowledge of the area. First, she drove to her new office and looked it over thoroughly, even peeked in the window of the locked front door. The sign on the door confirmed that they weren't open on Sunday. After two more hours of viewing luxurious homes, quaint businesses, and quite a few churches, she chanced upon a marina. She had to stop and look at the boats before she ended the day.

She walked row upon row of wooden planks and thrilled at the variety of boats. She loved them all. They satisfied something inside her, a yearning she didn't quite understand, comparable to the feeling she experienced when she looked at the picture of her own boating day.

At one of the slips, Katherine came upon a midsized boat that apparently had full time occupants. *What would it be like to live on a boat?*

Further on, she found the charter boats. One had just come in for the day and the scalded fishermen looked new to the area, too. Their happy laughter told her they had enjoyed a great day, in spite of the painful sunburn. At once, she decided she must charter a boat, no matter what the cost. She owed herself the experience. She copied down names and numbers for future investigation. She also jotted down phone numbers from the occasional *for sale* signs she came across—just out of curiosity about boat prices.

A man stepped from the cabin of one boat and waved a greeting to her.

"Nice boat," she said in appreciation.

"Come aboard and have a look-see."

"Thank you, but I'm not a buyer, just a looker."

"Well, come have a look, then. That won't cost anything."

"I'd love to." She stepped eagerly aboard and felt the thrill of another day and another boat. "How large is it?"

"Forty-six feet. I've done extensive custom work in the cabin. I put in a completely new galley and installed a lavatory and shower in the head. Go on in and look as long as you like."

Katherine couldn't resist doing exactly that. It didn't take long to see the possibilities a small area could offer. "I'm amazed at how much you have in there, so perfect and so luxurious," she said when she came out of the cabin.

Her compliments prompted the man to show her more extras he had personally added. His asking price, though beyond her means, still sat considerably lower than what she had expected. It planted a seed in her mind for later consideration.

"Thank you again for showing it to me," she said as she left.

It is bigger than my apartment in some ways. He didn't waste an inch of space, yet it looks neat and comfortable. Someday, maybe, I'll buy a boat.

That evening, Katherine decided to visit the beach every morning, even if only for a few minutes. Early the next day she headed straight for the beach and parked in her usual spot. From the water's edge, she gazed out at the Gulf, now tranquil and tinted with gold. She stared until her eyes burned—until she had clearly imprinted the ocean picture in her mind. Finally, she pulled away and drove to the new job.

Her broker, a man in his fifties with sleek black hair, unquestionably fitted his 'Big Buzzy' nickname in both height and girth. His gaudy clothes proclaimed casualness foreign to Chicago business attire, and his dark eyes leered when she introduced herself as his new salesperson.

"My goodness, Miss Katherine, here already? This is fine...fine! Come with me. I'll show you around a little, and we'll find you a place to stay."

She smiled, but his manner left her wordless. In his car, they took a brief tour of Naples, which eventually culminated at a condominium complex.

"This is one of my newer developments."

With considerable difficulty, he removed his bulk from the low-built vehicle and walked with her to the building's elevator. They toured three models before they returned to the sales model.

"I planned to introduce you to your selling partner, Alice, but she won't be here until later. Most days, you'll sell condos at this location, but on Tuesdays you'll work as a secretary in my real estate office. You'll get at least every other weekend off, and any week that you have to work on the weekend, you'll get a weekday or two off. Now what do you think of my building? Do you think you can sell these homes?"

"They're certainly nice, and I like the floor plans. I'm sure they sell themselves."

He smiled his pleasure. "Later I'll show you my other buildings, but let's head back to the office now." He patted her on the shoulder and smiled again.

She sat stiffly and tried to look at the passing scenery with interest, but his very presence made her uncomfortable.

"You're all alone down here, a pretty girl like you? Did you bring a boyfriend with you from Chicago?" He patted her hand on the seat.

She edged closer to her door but tried to answer pleasantly. "I came alone."

"My, my, all alone. But this is a nice safe job, and

we'll look out for you, Miss Katherine."

"Thank you, Mr. Amano." She couldn't think of anything else to say.

"Buzzy—call me Buzzy. Everyone does. Or Big Buzzy, if you need to ask a favor." He laughed and winked at her.

Katherine hoped her misgivings didn't show on her face. She decided she would *never* call him Big Buzzy.

At the real estate office, he pulled up beside her car.

"Follow me in your car now, Katherine. We'll look at a rental that might do. If it suits you, you can stay and get settled."

She had expected an apartment, but he parked at a tiny guesthouse hidden behind a large, attractive frame house.

"The occupants of the main house travel a good part of the year, so you'll have plenty of privacy. You can walk to our office from here."

The guesthouse, though not as nice as her apartment in Chicago, had lower rent than she had expected to pay in this expensive tourist town.

"This will do perfectly."

"Fine, fine, Miss Katherine. Get yourself moved in and comfortable, and call me if you need anything. By the way, this week I'd like you to work in the office on Wednesday instead of Tuesday. That way you can work tomorrow at the condos and get used to things there. You should begin a real estate course here, too. You'll want your Florida license as soon as possible so you can handle all our listings and sales."

"I'll check into it." Finally alone, Katherine breathed a sigh of relief. She wasn't sure she liked her new boss. He had treated her like his personal property, and that made her uncomfortable. *I am in real estate for now, and I'll save as much money as I can. But I plan to find another career.*

She opened all the windows to air out the house, and then laughed at what she had done. No one in Chicago could do that at this time of year. The house wasn't first class, but its beautiful foliage and privacy made up for any lack. She gave the house a quick cleaning and moved in her few belongings.

Later, Katherine went to town for supplies and stopped to have the number changed on her cell phone. That action helped wipe out lingering remnants of fear about Chicago stalkers, or other elusive villains. She slept deeply and peacefully that night, and after a quick visit at the beach the next morning, she drove to her new job at the condos.

A friendly woman in a loose-fitting cotton suit greeted Katherine warmly. "I'm Alice, and I'm guessing you're my new sales partner. I sure am glad to have help. I've told Buzzy that one person can't handle this alone."

"Are there many units left?"

"Goodness, yes. The building's only been open for a week."

By day's end, Katherine was satisfied with the job and genuinely liked Alice. It helped to know she could stick out the job until she could plan another direction for her future.

Her complacency nose-dived the next morning when she burst into the real estate office and took her new boss by surprise. He and a young man with a handsome, surly face were engaged in a passionate argument. Both of them looked disturbed by her sudden entrance.

So much for getting to work early. I shouldn't have skipped my beach visit this morning.

Her boss eyed her suspiciously.

"Miss Katherine, did you want something?"

"Just work—and a desk would help, too," she said lightly and with what she hoped was a pleasant smile. "I work in the office today, you know."

The friendly Buzzy instantly came to the fore, but the younger man's heavy-lidded eyes glared at her. He didn't wait for an introduction, but stormed out of the office.

"That's my son, Johnny. He handles our commercial properties. Been having problems."

Katherine nodded. "Yes. Commercial listings can be a headache."

She didn't want him to know she had heard enough to realize the argument didn't involve real estate. Ill-tempered Johnny wanted more money, right away, and Daddy told him to wait. She was in no hurry to meet this tall, athletic version of Buzzy.

The ultra-friendly Buzzy draped his arm across her shoulders. "How do you like our little town? You don't miss Chicago yet, do you?" He didn't wait for an answer. "I'll find time soon to give you the grand tour. It will help you in your sales, and we can get better acquainted."

The arrival of sales associates saved Katherine from his further attentions.

Buzzy assigned her a desk, explained her duties, and left her to work. Near lunchtime, he called her into his office. "Miss Katherine, you have one other duty I forgot to mention."

"Yes?" She braced herself.

"On Friday evenings, after office hours, it will be your responsibility to come in and clean the office. Just vacuum and dust things so they're fresh for Monday. It should take about thirty minutes, and I'll pay you for a full extra hour. This job always falls to the newest person here," he added apologetically and handed her a ring of keys. "The blue ones are door keys, and this orange one's for the alarm. The alarm is set at both doors, so be sure to turn it off before you enter. Once you're inside, you can turn the alarm back on if it makes you feel safer. There's an inside switch by both doors for that purpose. I sometimes turn it on when I work here at night. Expect a loud test-buzz whenever you turn it on or off."

Her newest responsibility bothered her more than she cared to admit. She didn't mind work, not even menial tasks like cleaning up after everyone, but Buzzy's manner left her with a trapped feeling. *Oh well, this is only temporary. I'll soon find other work. I'm in Florida now and can stand anything for a while.*

Office business that day rolled along at a slow pace and left her plenty of time to contemplate the future. Her thoughts kept drifting back to the boats. With the coming weekend off, she could charter a boat for a day. She called the two numbers she had saved, but both boats had already booked parties.

Later that day, Katherine discovered a yellowed business card on the office bulletin board that advertised another charter boat, Miss Iris, and its owner, Dale Townsend. She noted the address and made plans to go there after work. At quitting time, she drove directly to the marina and found a charter sign halfway down the docks next to an older boat. It looked decidedly less luxurious than the ones she had seen on Sunday. She actually liked it better. The faded sign matched the information on her business card, and a man worked on the boat.

"Excuse me. Could you tell me the rate for chartering this boat for a day of fishing? I had hoped to get a boat for this Saturday or Sunday."

The man climbed out of the boat and removed his worn captain's hat to disclose thick, white hair and eyes that must have viewed thousands of sunsets.

"How many in your party, Ma'am?" he asked with a slow, pleasant drawl.

"Only me. I've never done this kind of fishing. I don't know anything about it."

"Ma'am, I can take you on Saturday for half-rate. I have a party of two goin' out in the morning. Plenty of room for you. They've done a heap of fishin' so you can watch them to see how it's done. There's nothin' much to it, though."

"Do I need to bring anything?"

"Your own lunch and drinks. We leave out of here early—five thirty."

"Thank you. I'll be here." Katherine felt like skipping back to her car and was still in that eager mood come morning as she dressed for work. Although a trip to the filling station ate up most of her spare time, she hurried to the beach for a quick visit.

No cars had parked at her special beach location. She kicked off her shoes and ran down to the water's edge like someone greeting an old friend too long neglected. She dipped her hands in the sun-glazed surf and threw sprays of water into the air. That felt so satisfying that she twirled around and began to kick water in every direction until she risked real danger of soaking her work clothes. She laughed at her foolishness.

There was no time for a walk. She waved goodbye to the view and ran back up the beach feeling more than a little silly.

A green Jeep was now parked beside her car. The single occupant hadn't gotten out, but he was looking in her direction. No doubt, he had seen her juvenile display. He'd probably also seen her Illinois license tag and had laughed at the silly tourist. His tanned arm rested on the sill of his open window. Yes, he had laughed. She could see the smile still on his face.

Katherine got into her car. What did it matter if someone laughed at her? Maybe she should have said hello. He looked familiar, and she had met quite a few people in the last few days. That notion increased her uneasiness, and she sped away amidst a fresh wave of embarrassment.

4

Her days flew by and Friday evening arrived too soon. Rather than clean the office around late working associates, she waited until six o'clock when no people were present before she attempted the task.

She had barely started on the job before Buzzy breezed in. A more predatory Buzzy. She flew from one duty to the next, and she kept a vacuum cleaner between the two of them whenever possible. She skipped his private office and gave him no opportunity to pursue what so obviously filled his mind. He approached her while she put away the vacuum.

"Miss Katherine, it's not necessary for you to wear office clothes when you come here to clean. I'm sure shorts would feel more comfortable, and I hate to see you work this vigorously after a whole day at the condos. Take all the time you want, there's no hurry. No one will come in on a Friday evening."

"Actually, I *need* to hurry. I have plans for tonight and don't want to be late," she said with feigned naiveté.

That curbed his advances and it took only a minute to finish and call a hurried goodbye.

This will never work out. What will I do next Friday? One thing for sure, I'll lock the doors and set the alarm so at least I'm warned.

Although she slept restlessly, she arrived at the *Miss Iris* before anyone else. She had tucked food and drinks into one small ice chest and had worn the most comfortable and covering clothes she could find.

Two middle-aged men drove up as Captain Dale arrived. Everyone was friendly and polite, and she began to feel less concerned about her greenness. When the *Miss Iris* entered the Gulf waters, Katherine became too excited to fish. Most of the morning she rode on the bow and watched the boat cut through the water. Later in the day, she tried fishing. Everyone helped, and she had some success. When she tired of that pursuit, she took a seat beside Captain Dale and studied his every move.

"Ma'am, would you take over here while I fix a couple of rods?"

He stepped back from the wheel as if such a request was commonplace. She glanced out ahead and then back at him, not sure that she had heard him right.

"I've never run a boat."

"Here, take the wheel and keep her headin' straight on. Stay about the same distance from the shore. You'll be fine."

She moved to the helm, almost shaky in her excitement as she took hold of the wheel. It didn't steer like her car. She constantly overcorrected, but soon managed to keep a reasonably straight course and began to enjoy it. The captain paid her no attention and busied himself with other tasks.

"Captain Dale, a boat coming up on our right is about to cross in front of us. Maybe you'd better take over, now."

"That's our starboard side," he explained and took the wheel again. "They have the right of way. If she were comin' from the other side, you'd have it...but

31

don't ever trust that if you're operatin' a boat. Half of these boaters don't know what they're doin'."

"Are we very far out now?" she asked and studied the distant shoreline.

"I'd say about a mile and a half."

"Do you have instruments to tell you that or is it just from experience?"

"When you can set your bearings on something solid, you can usually tell the distance. Can you see the houses on shore well enough to count their windows?"

"Yes." She shaded her eyes and squinted towards the shoreline.

"Can you see the windows clearly and can you count the trees?"

"Not quite." She studied the shore for a few more seconds. "Almost, but not quite."

"That makes us about a mile and a half out. If you could count the trees, it would be about a mile. If you could *barely* count the windows, it would be about two miles."

"How about three miles," she asked and laughed.

"You'd only be able to see where the water and shore meet."

"That's great," she said enthusiastically.

"Yes, ma'am. Unless it's foggy, or dark, or raining, or you're out where you can't see any land. It can get trickier."

"Do *you* always know your location when there's no land in sight?"

"I surely don't. The finest instruments and charts can fail you, at times."

She began to realize the seriousness of operating a boat. She stayed beside him until the *Miss Iris* pulled into the slip that afternoon. In spite of her prevention measures, she was sunburned. She staggered onto the dock and watched proudly as they unloaded the day's catch.

A few people gathered around to watch, and she wanted to point at the fish and say, "I caught some of them. See that big kingfish…" She could now relate to the pride she had seen in other's faces after a day of fishing. Although most of the fish went to Captain Dale, she and the two men did take a few.

"Captain Dale, I have next Thursday off. Do you already have a party booked or could I have that day?" She asked breathlessly, brandishing a kingfish in one hand and her ice chest in the other.

A slow grin spread over his face.

"No ma'am, nothin' set for Thursday. You'll probably be the only party, but I'll give you a good rate. Weekdays I charge less, anyhow."

"Thank you. I'll see you then."

She waved goodbye to her two new fishing friends and climbed into her car. *I am most certainly insane*, she thought blissfully. *I shouldn't spend the money, but I have to go again.*

On her way home, she stopped at the library and chose some boating books. The day at sea had implanted some vague ideas regarding her future.

In the morning, she drove to a church she had seen a couple of blocks from where the *Miss Iris* docked. It felt strange attending a new church where she didn't know anyone, but everyone was so friendly she soon relaxed.

The small, old-fashioned church lay so close to the bay she could smell the flowers and salt air through the half-open windows. That Sunday's message on giving thanks, thrilled her with its fitness for celebrating her first full week in Naples. As the service progressed, she added a new reason for feeling thankful—on her very first try, she'd found a church home and already felt less alone in the world.

When she walked to her car, she noticed a weathered, blue sedan parked a short ways down from the church parking lot. The person in the driver's seat reminded her of her broker's son, Johnny. At that instant he looked up, and Johnny's glance met hers just as he drove off. She wished she hadn't looked. He hadn't been in church, and there was no one with him. Why had he parked there?

By the time, she showed up at the condos the next morning, the memory of Johnny had fallen behind in the wake of her wonderful boat ride.

"Good morning, Alice. You beat me to work. I stopped by the beach and couldn't leave. It's sublime this morning, so blue and still."

"Are you always this exuberant and sunburned, or just on Mondays?"

Katherine laughed. "I fished on a charter boat all day Saturday. That's the reason for the sunburn. The exuberance is because I think I've made a big decision."

"It isn't a decision if you're still *thinking* about it," Alice reminded.

"Then I've *made* a decision—a rather *terrifyingly* big decision."

"It must be. You haven't even poured yourself a cup of coffee, yet. Wasn't your move from Chicago to Florida decision enough to last you for a while? You haven't decided to move back, have you?"

"Actually, I may make it impossible to move back. I intend to buy a boat—a cabin cruiser."

"They must pay you more than they pay me." She smiled and took a drink of coffee. "Go on, I have to hear this."

"I probably can't afford it, and I haven't found *my* boat yet, but when I do find it and buy it, I'll be too broke to go anywhere, least of all, back to Chicago. I'll probably need *two* jobs to pay for it."

"If it's that important to you, don't let anyone talk you out of it—not even me. I expect a ride as soon as you get it."

The rest of Katherine's plan, still in the formulating stage, involved vague ideas about using the boat commercially, the way Captain Dale did. Though it sounded preposterous, even to her, she could hardly wait to get her own boat and chalk up some experience.

During all her spare time the next couple of days, she called on ads in the newspaper, viewed boats at private docks, and finally drove from marina to marina in her search.

Johnny and his blue sedan didn't show up again, but a new vehicle began to appear surprisingly often — a green Jeep like the one parked at the beach the morning she acted like a kindergartener. Evidently, her Chicago accident had left her paranoid. It was time to forget cars and concentrate on boats if she ever expected to own one.

By the time she boarded the *Miss Iris* for her next outing, Katherine had a thorough knowledge of boat prices. She had found quite a few affordable boats, but not one that fit her exactly. When she settled on the seat beside Captain Dale, she knew this would be the last outing she could afford. She planned to ask many questions.

"How old were you when you first ran a boat?" she asked as they headed down the bay.

"Ma'am, I was just a kid, but I never worked steady on boats until I was thirteen. That's when I quit school to help my daddy. There wasn't much charterin' back then, not much of *anything* back then, so we fished when we had no parties to take out."

"I guess Naples looked a lot different then."

"Just a spot along the Tamiami Trail, and most everyone went to Fort Myers to shop. I attended school barefoot in those days. You'd never see *that* now."

"I guess you've seen quite a few changes since you were a child."

"Yes ma'am. I've seen piles of money come into the area, and that's what changed it." He drifted off in thought for a few minutes. "I'm not so young, you know." He laughed. "I don't work much anymore, but I probably know this area as well, or better, than most anyone around. The channels, the mangrove islands, the currents—those don't change as much as things on shore."

"Like prices? I guess you could get a lot more boat for your money back when you bought the *Miss Iris*." She grew embarrassed at her poor attempt to steer their conversation to boat prices. "I want to buy a boat—a cabin cruiser like this one if I can find one I can afford," she finally blurted out. "I've looked at boats all week."

"Do you plan on financin' it?" He asked in his same easygoing manner.

"I have savings, but I'll have to finance some of it. None of the boats I looked at fit what I want."

"Don't go and buy somethin', like a boat, unless you get exactly what you want. You don't buy a boat every day. You'll probably keep it a while."

His advice amused Katherine. This old sea captain sounded like her when she showed clients a house or condo.

"I intend to keep it a long time. That's why I'm so picky. I've checked all the local marinas and called on all the ads I could find. Will I need to go out of this area? Where would you look if you were in the market for a boat like this one?"

"Well, let me see, now. If you're lookin' for an old, beat-up boat like this, you could always buy mine. It's been for sale over a year and—"

"For sale? What would you do if you sold it?"

"I passed retirement age quite a spell ago, and I'd still have my little motor boat for fishin'. That's all I need." He gave her a craggy smile and quoted his asking price.

She stared at him wordless.

Of course, the boat had a few years on it and was made of wood, not fiberglass, but his price was half the price of similar boats she had investigated.

"The *Miss Iris* would be perfect." She tried to keep the thrill out of her voice.

"She needs work. Do you plan to use her, or did you want somethin' to admire and pour money into?"

"I'd like to take parties out like you do, someday when I have more experience. I know it sounds unreasonable."

"More reasonable than speedin' around for the sport of it and wasting gas."

"No speedboats for me." She laughed. "I just want a fishing boat."

"Well, she's fine for that. The motor's good, but the hull needs work. Has a couple of small soft spots and leaks, needs scraped and painted. I've been meanin' to pull her—just haven't gotten around to it. If you're interested, you should bring a mechanic around to look her over. He might find problems I don't know about."

"I'm interested." Even through its accumulation of grime and scars, she could see the boat's possibilities.

"If you mean to become a boat owner, you need experience captainin' worse than you need fishin' lessons today. Take over the helm, and I'll try and teach you everything I know before we head back in." He chuckled and moved away from the wheel.

By day's end, Katherine had gotten the hang of operating a large boat on open water and in the bay. Only when she tried to back the boat into its slip, did she realize how much she didn't know. "Will I ever be able to dock it properly?" she asked after her third try.

"You're not used to it. When you get familiar with the currents and the way the boat handles, you'll have no trouble at all." He sat back in a fishing chair and fiddled with a box of tackle until she finally brought it into its slip. "Now take care of your lines. I'd help, but you may need to handle the job unassisted, sometime. Make sure you leave enough slack to allow for the tide."

When she had tied it to his satisfaction, she helped hose it down and set up an appointment for a mechanic to come by the next day. She couldn't help taking one last look at it before she headed home.

That evening two commission checks were in the mail. Adding those to her savings, she could pay most of the boat's price and have money left for insurance and incidentals. All she needed was the mechanics report, so she left work early the next day to accompany the mechanic as he examined the boat.

"You should take care of those leaks as soon as possible. The engine's sound. That's a big motor you got there—more power than you'll probably ever need unless you're outrunning a gale."

"Something I hope I never have to do."

When the mechanic finished his inspection, Captain Dale came aboard and showed her some of the equipment.

"The bilge pump is manual. Remember to turn it on every two days and pump the bilge dry, that is, until you get the leaks patched. Here's the auxiliary pump—in case you get caught in heavy seas and ship too much water, or in case the other pump quits on you. As far as I know, everything on the boat works satisfactorily, but later on you may want to modernize some of the equipment."

After they finished, she drove Captain Dale to his house only half a block from the docks. He led her into a large back yard, heavily hedged by tropical growth and completely private from any nearby dwellings. A small skiff lay upside down on the yard near the water.

"I generally leave my car at home and walk to the boat. There's my other boat." He pointed to a sporty, speedboat tied to his private dock. "The canal here is too shallow for the *Miss Iris*."

"This canal runs into the bay, then?"

"It connects the bay a short ways over from where the *Miss Iris* sits. This is the second inlet on the right when you head out of the marina towards the pass."

They went into his house, and she met his wife, Iris, a warmly shy woman.

"Would ya like some tea?" Iris asked with a more pronounced drawl than Dale.

"Yes, thank you," Katherine said and took a seat at a small, kitchen table. Iris brought her a glass of sweetened iced tea, which surprised her. Too new from wintry Chicago, she had expected a cup of hot tea.

"Were you born in Naples?" Katherine asked her while Captain Dale went to find boat documents.

"My family all come from Marco. Like Dale's family, ours was a fishin' family. Near about all of Marco lived on fish in them days." Iris volunteered, standing by the table with her hands clasped in front of her.

Captain Dale returned and showed Katherine the papers.

"If you'll insure the boat, I'll finance the balance at five percent interest. I think that's better than the bank would offer."

"It's certainly better than the bank. If you're satisfied, you have a deal. What day would you like to finalize everything?"

"Any day next week, after Monday. I'll need to use it until then."

"I could meet you at the bank Wednesday at noon. We can have everything notarized, and I'll pay you with cash, a money order, or any way you want."

"A check's fine. Now you just come by anytime you have a question," he added when they shook hands.

Driving away from his house, the enormity of the commitment was daunting. But deep down, she didn't regret it.

Later that evening she remembered she must clean the office. To avoid another unannounced visit by Buzzy, she walked to wok so that no telltale car would give her presence away. She entered the door, reset the alarm, and closed the blinds in the large open section where the associate's desks sat. She vacuumed and cleaned that area and the kitchen alcove with only the aid of a flashlight.

Buzzy's office had no windows, so she closed the door and turned on his light. The accumulation of dust suggested that his office had rarely been cleaned. While moving the papers on his desk to clean it, a newspaper clipping caught her attention. It was from a Chicago paper, one she knew well, so she picked it up for a closer look.

It was the top one third of a page, and she didn't see anything of interest—only small sections of continued articles that had appeared on earlier pages. The other side of the clipping contained a large advertisement for a Chicago bank. It showed pictures of all their employees and their respective departments.

She returned it to the desk only to pick it up again.

It was the bank Lloyd's office used for many of their deals—and Laura's bank. She found Mr. Pinkston's face with his name below. Glancing at the other people, the face of Johnny Amano suddenly stared out. But no—the paper called him *Jack Evans*. No one could mistake Johnny's face, not with those distinctive eyes.

*Jack Evan*s. The name sounded familiar. She had seen it written somewhere, but couldn't recall ever hearing it. Johnny's picture being in the ad would explain Buzzy saving it. She had seen them together enough to note Buzzy's paternal affection for his big boy.

Something wasn't right. The clipping was dated only a week before she left Chicago. With no time for deliberation right then, she hastily copied the clipping on the office printer and returned the original to Buzzy's desk. She took time to disarrange his papers as they had looked before her ministrations.

At eight o'clock, back in the privacy of her house, she studied the clipping and tried to remember where she had seen the name Jack Evans. It somehow made her think of Laura's problem, so she got out the old file. The top paper was the bank statement signed by Pinkston that Lloyd had given her. She looked no further. Jack Evans was the name of the bank employee who made the error. It didn't make sense, but there he was in the ad wearing Johnny's face.

On her laptop, she found the bank's website and a page of employee pictures, but no Jack Evans. Maybe Laura could look into it for her. Laura worked for the city and might have a directory or some resource that would shed light on this. She might even recall the man's face if she saw a picture of him. She dialed Laura's number and waited. Johnny's eyes seemed to peer into hers as she stared at the picture, but Laura's vivacious greeting dispelled the vision.

"Kay, where are you? Are you still in Florida? I got your postcard, and then you dropped off the edge of the world. Are you OK?"

"I'm in Naples, and I'm fine. I'm sorry I waited so long to call you. Everything happened so fast—my moving to Florida and the new job. I saw the emails you sent, but I didn't want to answer until I had decided for sure about my future. I guess I decided that today."

"You didn't give me an address, and your cell phone number didn't work."

"I changed the number, and I'll email you my

address. I'm happily settled in a nice place, and I have a good job selling condos. How are your house repairs going?"

"Perfectly wonderful. You should see it."

Katherine waited until Laura had finished her lengthy discourse about her house's renovation before she brought up what filled her mind.

"Laura, I need a favor. I need information on the man your bank fired because he didn't pay your insurance." She couldn't keep her gaze from drifting to the picture again.

"Kay, please! You promised you'd drop the whole thing. I know you're responsible for our good fortune, but I don't want to make anyone angry—at least not until I'm back in my house."

"Don't worry, Laura. It's nothing to do with your house trouble. I just need a description of the man if you can get it."

"I don't think they ever told me his name, and I doubt I've ever seen him. Why?"

"I think the man works at my real estate office here." A chill traveled up her back in spite of the warmth of the night.

"Wow. That's strange."

"His name's Jack Evans. I need a description of him and any information about him you can dig up discreetly. I'll email you a newspaper ad that pictures his face."

"I'll try, Katherine. Oh, by the way, your old boss, Lloyd Lucas, called today."

"I'm glad he's still looking out for your interests." She turned the picture face down and tried to forget Johnny for a minute.

"He called about you. He wanted your address,

and he asked if I'd talked with you recently. I told him we hadn't talked since you left, and I didn't have your address."

"Is that all he called about?"

"That was it."

"I wonder why he called you to ask that. He has my address and my new phone number. He even mailed me some checks."

"Kind of weird, but honestly, that's all he asked. He didn't even ask about our house repairs. And speaking of that, I was just getting ready to take some new curtains over to it. I'll take some pictures while I'm there so you can see what's going on. I have to run now. My guy's beeping at me to hurry." In spite of her impatient husband, Laura managed to talk another five minutes about her house repairs before she finally said goodbye.

5

Katherine rose early Monday morning so she could have some beach time before work. During her walk, she tried to picture her boat on the horizon. On her return trip she noticed a surf fisherman.

"Hi," he said quietly in response to her nod. The cutoffs, tan skin, and dark hair, set against the background of endless sea, were an eye-catching combination. He looked to be in his mid-thirties.

She watched as he made long casts into the gulf. It looked like fun. She decided to buy fishing equipment and try it. She couldn't very well start a charter business and take parties out fishing if she was a novice, and the beach offered plenty of room for practice. At least she wouldn't get her line tangled in other's lines the way people on the pier often did.

When she returned to her car, the green Jeep was parked beside it. Obviously he owned it and fished at this spot regularly. She glanced at him again. The Jeep fit him—fit him the way that empty beach and rolling surf did, and she lingered a minute more and watched.

During her lunch break, she visited a hardware store and found that her fishing experience on the *Miss Iris* would help in choosing gear. With the added advice of a sales clerk, she was outfitted with a moderately heavy rod and reel, and a tackle box.

"Now I need fishing line, all sizes of hooks and sinkers, leader wire, pliers, wire cutters, a gaff hook, a bait bucket, and a fish stringer. And treble hooks."

He laughed. "You should get some spoons and other lures, too."

"Pile them up—anything I might need. I'm going fishing!"

The rest of the day at the condos crept by. She and Alice sipped coffee and stared out the window at a spring rain that seemed to have chased all the buyers away.

"Have you been with this real estate office very long?"

"About two years. I do nothing but show condos. When this building sells out, they'll put me in another." Alice got up and refilled both of their cups.

"Do the Amanos do that much building?"

"Buzzy does," Alice said crisply. "I don't know what Johnny does. I thought he'd moved away, but now he's back."

"I met him on my second day of work. He seemed...unpleasant."

"I would have used a stronger word to describe him, but his daddy dotes on him. The only son thing, you know."

Katherine couldn't help pondering over the Jack Evans/Johnny Amano situation. Too many *whys* drifted through her life lately. With no plausible explanation for any of them, her imagination ran wild. Just as she got ready to leave for the day, she received a text from Laura: *Jack Evans gone from bank. Moved away. More info later.*

When Katherine headed to the beach the following morning, she brought her new rod, rigged for surf fishing. She even wore a bathing suit so she could wade into the water to fish, but when she saw the green Jeep parked there, she decided that no one should witness her first casting attempts. Reluctantly she left the new gear in her car and set off for a walk.

The green-Jeep man kneeled on the beach by his open tackle box, and when she passed by, he looked up. "Hi again," he said and smiled

"Good morning. Nice day for the beach." Katherine returned his smile and continued walking. *"No chance he's single. He is much too good-looking.* She laughed at herself. At least someone sparked her interest. In Chicago she rarely met anyone who could make her look twice, but now she felt like anything could happen.

The water washing around her feet felt warmer than usual, warm enough to risk a swim. She plunged in and instantly gasped at its chilliness. The initial shock soon wore off, and she enjoyed splashing around in the waves. When she glanced up the beach at some noisy seagulls, she caught the Jeep man's intense scrutiny in her direction. He quickly turned away.

He was gone when she returned to her car. She glanced at her new tackle. There was no time to try it, but she could go to the pier after work and fish around the pilings.

Office work and the business of the boat purchase kept her so busy she didn't arrive at the pier until late. She hurried to the bait house for shrimp, and at a short section of vacant rail, she lowered the bait into the water and waited patiently. Many nibbles and jerks later she landed a small pinfish, and offered it to a man fishing nearby who used live bait.

After a while she tossed her line out a short distance, set a light drag, and leaned her rod against the rail so she could sit and enjoy the night's enchantment. Only a few people remained on the pier—the serious ones who came to fish. She breathed deeply of the salt air, rich with the fresh tang of fish and ocean. The stars came out and the only sounds were the whizzing of fishing lines, the plunks of bait or lures entering the water, and the lapping of water on the pilings below.

The dark water, beautiful with shimmering fluorescence, teemed with life. Deep in its depths, she could see the phosphorescence from schools of fish as they passed below. Now and then, she could make out the shape of a huge fish cruising into the shallow water near the beach, and rows of large snook waited in layers at the edge of the pier's shadow. Occasionally one or two would break away to feed, but seldom on the baited hooks or lures that were thrown near to tempt them.

Eventually she landed a sheepshead, which she kept. Her fascination increased as the night wore on. Although strikes were few, whenever anyone did hook something sizeable, there ensued a general tumult and scramble by those nearby to reel in their lines and get out of the way. Too often the fish would break the line or cut it off on the sharp pilings. One man landed a large redfish, and there were a few catches of smaller fish, but the highlight of the night was when someone landed a nurse shark. After that, the night grew quieter, but it remained a magical world, and she couldn't pull away.

At three o'clock Katherine finally crawled into bed, and it seemed like only minutes later the alarm went off. She groaned and pulled the covers up, almost persuaded to skip the beach walk and get an extra hour of sleep. But this was boat day—no day to sleep in.

No vehicles had parked at her beach avenue. Suddenly a walk on the beach seemed like a massive chore to her weary body. Even a session with her new fishing gear didn't tempt her, especially since she had worn her good clothes.

It wasn't time for work, so she rolled down her car windows, let down the back of her seat, and tried to take a brief nap. Two minutes later, she put her seat back up, pushed the armrest out of the way, and lay down across the front seats with her purse for a pillow. That put her out of sight, yet she could see the top of a coconut palm through her windshield. Breezes blew through her windows and drowsiness soon turned to sleep.

When consciousness sluggishly returned, a suntanned face with questioning eyes had replaced the palm tree. Startled, she recognized the green-Jeep man. He must have parked beside her and glanced in. Thoroughly awake now, she felt like a bum on a park bench and couldn't decide whether to close her eyes and pretend she hadn't seen him, or jump up and say something witty—but what?

"Good morning. Nice day for a nap." He smiled down at her. His tone seemed to straddle the halfway mark between friendly and smart-aleck.

Katherine sat upright in the seat, but too late—he had gone on. All she could see was his back as he carried his gear down to the beach. Had that been a mocking light in his eyes or was it just her imagination? Why did his eyes look so familiar? Where had she seen that expression before, those same hazel eyes? Finally, her embarrassment fled as good sense took over. People napped in their vehicles all the time, and now it was time for work.

At noon, Captain Dale met her in the bank, and a painless, but terrifying fifteen minutes later, she stepped out into the sunshine a full-fledged boat owner.

"Come by this evenin' if you can. I'll try and dig out some more papers you may need," he suggested before he left.

The financial arrangements satisfied her completely. She could pay her monthly boat payment, dock rent, and still have money left for house rent—*if* she decided to keep her little cottage. She wanted to see if she could live on the boat. It probably wouldn't do for long term, but she wanted to try it for a while. At least, it would save money if she had to find another job.

Two other boats at her marina had full time occupants, though they docked at the other side. If they could do it, why couldn't she? Her slip already had electric and water hookups, and she had her cell phone for calls.

Iris met her at the door that evening when she came by for the boat papers.

"Come in, Miss Gale, and sit a spell. Dale went out, but he'll be back shortly."

"Thank you. I just came by for some papers." Katherine took a seat and glanced around the homey room. "You have a lovely home."

The open windows let in gentle breezes from off the bay, and thin, white muslin curtains framed the yard's lush growth.

"Thank ya, ma'am. I like it here. It's kinda quiet, and I like bein' near the water." Iris seemed timid, but she answered questions readily enough.

"I understand. If you grew up in a fishing family, you've probably always been around the water. I envy you."

"Envy me?" Iris seemed taken aback and looked out the window for a minute. "I'm real glad Dale sold the boat to someone who loves the water."

"Do you mind that he sold it? Will you miss going out on it with him?"

"Land sakes, no. I been wishin' he'd sell it all these years. I never go out with him. When I want to fish, I fish from my dock or sometimes take the skiff out a ways. That's enough for me. Would ya like to see our dock while we're waitin' on Dale?"

"That would be nice," Katherine followed Iris into the back yard.

"Dale built me this stand to clean my fish. Sometimes I clean fish for his parties when they need it. It's real handy since Dale hooked me up electric and water."

"I haven't cleaned many fish, and I'm very unskilled at it. Maybe you could show me the proper way sometime."

"You just bring 'em by next time ya have some. I have an electric filletin' knife, and I believe I'm faster 'n most. I've done it near about all my life."

Captain Dale joined them at the dock and handed her an envelope full of papers. "These are owner's manuals for the stove, refrigerator, and some of the instruments. I was thinkin' you should have another day on the water. I never showed you the instruments, and you could use more practice. When's your next free day?"

"I'm off this Saturday—if you can spare the time."

"Yes'm, shore I can. You're gonna take me on a

fishin' trip, and we'll split the catch. I'll see you Saturday morning. I have to go now."

Katherine and Iris enjoyed a long chat after Captain Dale left, and were well acquainted by the time Katherine rose to leave. Before Katherine climbed into her car, she turned and smiled at Iris, who waited to wish her goodbye. "I've been attending the church on the next block over, and I thought I'd try their service tonight. I'm new there and would love some company. Would you care to come with me or do you attend somewhere else?"

Although Iris had become more outgoing as the evening progressed, she seemed frightened at the prospect of a church service. "I—I can't tonight...maybe another time. It *is* a good church...a real good little church." She started to go into the house, but suddenly turned back to Katherine. "Could ya wait a minute? I have somethin' for ya." She returned with a small jar and handed it to Katherine. "Some guava jelly I made. I have two trees of guavas and always make more than Dale and I can use. Come again, now, ya hear?"

Katherine drove past the boat docks before she went to church. She had to look at the *Miss Iris*—her *Miss Iris! It's beautiful. Rough and worn and beautiful—like the person it's named after.*

She saw the unplumbed depths in the quiet, reclusive wife of Dale, the wistfulness behind the broad, weather-beaten face. Katherine liked the woman's natural, down-to-earth manner and hoped they would become close friends.

6

When Katherine's ever-faithful alarm startled her awake, she felt very different from yesterday's bold woman who gave away most of her life savings for an old wooden fishing boat. Uneasy and a little scared, she questioned her rash actions, worried about them for a few minutes, and finally took them to God: *Lord, I thought I had your blessing on my big decision, but if I didn't listen to you closely enough, please bless my actions and help me to go forward in your will.*

She prayed until her fears and doubts vanished, until she knew that God would partner with her in the new venture. When she rose from her knees to face the day, joy and confidence swept over her. Yesterday had changed her life. She now owned a large fishing boat. However inept and inexperienced, she was captain of the *Miss Iris*. The realization gave her a spunky mood change. She would go to the beach as usual that morning, and even if the green-Jeep man were there she would still fish.

Katherine chose clothes she could wear to work— white cotton pants and a thin, stretchy, sleeveless top with yellow daisies. The mirror hinted that the sunny top flattered her figure. *Not bad—the perfect top for casting practice,* she told the deceitful, blushing image.

The beach was deserted. She carried her fishing gear down the beach in the opposite direction from where the Jeep man had fished. While she stood at the water's edge, she tried a couple of experimental overhead casts. They both resulted in backlashes and required frustrating work to straighten the line. More determined than ever, she rolled her pants to the middle of her calves and waded in further. Her next casts plunked into the water only a few feet in front of her. A dozen or more of the same drove her to desperate measures. She let out more line, gripped the rod tightly with both hands, and gave a mighty heave.

"Ouch!" Katherine gasped, startled by the sudden sharp pain in the back of her thigh. The treble hook had made a wicked slice across her flesh and imbedded itself in her pants. She reached back to disengage it.

Alien fingers already attempted to do the job.

Her startled jump not only triggered her loss of balance and awkward plunge into the ocean, but also caused the hook to rake across her unfortunate rescuer's palm as she knocked him into the swirling water beside her.

Jeep-man rose dripping from his briny bath. He carelessly wiped his bleeding hand on his jeans while she continued to flounder in the rolling surf. With his other hand, he pulled her to her feet and without saying a word, he worked until he freed the lure from her pants. Deep-set hazel eyes looked sympathetically into her eyes. "That's a bad scratch. That couldn't have felt pleasant."

She blinked and tears threatened.

"I have a medicine bag in my Jeep. Let's put a wrap on that before you bleed anymore," he stated, matter-of-factly.

Nervously, Katherine tried to make light of the situation. She gestured towards his wounded hand. "It looks as if I've caught *you* with my bad cast," she said, half-laughing, half-hysterical. She immediately saw the possible double meaning of her words, but it was too late to withdraw them.

"You tried, anyway."

Katherine's face warmed and she knew she was blushing. Feeling like a scolded child, she followed him to his Jeep. Among the clutter of fishing gear, oxygen tanks, swim fins, masks, and sundry other items, he came up with a professional looking medicine case. "Will that pant leg roll up?" He didn't wait for her reply, but rolled it without her assistance. "This looks deep. You're lucky the hook didn't imbed in your leg." He treated the long laceration with antiseptic and bandaged it securely. "Keep medicine on this. You don't want it to become infected. If you take care of it, you probably won't need to see a doctor, and since you've already rinsed your pants in cold water..." he grinned, noting her dripping wet condition, "you won't have any blood stains on your pants." He rolled her pant leg back down, and then looked at her with interest.

"Thank you." She hadn't meant for it to sound so cool and haughty, but his proximity disconcerted her. She tried to smile.

"Do you want casting lessons now?" he asked and smiled back.

She nearly choked as she restrained her temper and swallowed a sharp retort. "I'm late for w-work." She climbed into the car and backed halfway out when she remembered her tackle on the beach.

Her aquatic-knight leaned against his Jeep with his arms folded and watched her with an amused look as she pulled back into the parking spot.

She rushed to retrieve her gear and thought she heard his mellow laugh. On her return trip, she had a curt remark ready, but he gave her no chance to use it.

He unloaded gear from his Jeep and totally ignored her.

"That's all right with me," she mumbled as she drove away.

The next morning she decided to skip her beach visit. Her leg hurt, and she wasn't ready for Mr. Green Jeep, yet. She wasn't ready for Buzzy, either. He was at the sales condo when she arrived.

"Hi, Katherine. I haven't seen much of you lately, so I came out to check how my new little saleslady was getting on. You've done fine work here. Don't miss your old home yet, do you?"

She studied his smiling face. Why had he bothered to come to the condos and ask such a question when she had been in the office three days ago? Had he hoped to catch her alone since Alice wouldn't come in until noon?

"I've forgotten Chicago altogether." She gave a cool-friendly smile.

He approached too close for comfort.

While she contemplated how ladylike it would look if she jumped over the counter, some prospective buyers wandered in and saved her from any unpleasantness.

Leisurely Katherine showed them the condos and invited questions. Finally, she invented questions to prolong the showing. When she returned, Buzzy had left, but a new trial awaited her in the form of Johnny.

Although he had never said more than two words before, he now treated her like an old friend. "How's the real estate game treating you? Slower here than in

Chicago, I'll bet. You plan to stay?"

Katherine wanted to laugh. A younger, hipper, and definitely more muscular version of Buzzy had just asked her the same identical questions Buzzy had asked.

"I like it here. I'd never move back north again." Her answer seemed to please and encourage Johnny.

"That's some classy outfit you're wearing. It brightens up the place. Say, I'm about to go for lunch. Care to come along?"

"I'm sorry, Johnny. I've already made lunch plans. Maybe we can do it some other time."

"Next time you're free, I'll show you a good place to eat," he announced taking acceptance for granted, and sauntered off.

She breathed a sigh of relief. Johnny's presence bothered her, represented an unknown factor, though he did seem rather harmless. Maybe he had a crush on her. It would probably get worse now that he had grown bold enough to talk with her.

Katherine decided she wouldn't clean the office that night and risk one of the Amanos walking in on her. Though neither man had acted inappropriately, her experience and instincts tolled an alarm each time one of them came near her. Why invite a possible, awkward confrontation that could end her job before she secured a new one? She would get up before daylight, walk to the office, and clean it before anyone came around.

Very early the next morning Katherine crept into the office through the back door of the kitchen. She hurriedly vacuumed the main room, working more by feel than by the feeble light that shone through the windows. When she had completed that job, she noiselessly dumped all the trash into the outside dumpster. She had just reset the alarm at the back door and put a fresh plastic bag into the kitchen garbage receptacle when the front door buzzer sounded.

Katherine slid her purse strap over her shoulder and prepared to scurry out the back before someone could reset the alarm. Since no lights were on, no one would know of her presence if she left quietly. Her hand had started to turn the knob when the second buzzer sounded. Voices followed and she paused in uncertainty. If she left now, the alarm would sound, and if she turned it off, it would buzz. She had no choice but to walk into the main room and make her presence known.

"No more killing, Johnny, or you'll get us killed." Katherine froze as Buzzy's angry voice cut the stillness. "You could have ruined everything. From now on, don't do anything unless you're following his orders or mine. Do you hear me? Do you understand?"

With her heart performing acrobatics, Katherine pulled her hand back from the light switch she had almost flipped and stood in silent horror. If either of them walked to the far side of the main office, they would see her. She looked around for an avenue of escape—any place where she could hide.

Johnny mumbled something incoherently, and she felt certain they headed her way. Almost frantic, she scanned her surroundings again and saw her only hope, the plastic garbage barrel.

Swiftly and silently, she climbed in and pulled the lid on after her. Darkness closed in on her, and she wondered how long the limited oxygen would last. The lid overlapped the barrel's edge by about four inches and the plastic bag helped seal off any chance of fresh air seeping in. She wished the lid fitted more loosely, wished the barrel was larger, wished she was anywhere but there. She could hear everything. It sounded like they had come into the kitchen.

"If he ever found out why I sent you up there, we'd both be dead. I lied for you. I convinced him you wanted to get in the Chicago end of the business. Now I'm tired of lying for you. That fool trick you pulled here for forty grand could have blown everything. This town is too small for such exploits."

"I got more than that, and I needed some new wheels." Johnny's surly voice now sounded louder than Buzzy's. "I've been taking all the risks here, and I couldn't even afford a decent car. Besides, I told you nothing would come of it. I did things right. You didn't need to send me up there."

"That was a precaution...in case you didn't do things right. I sent you up there to protect you, but I never would have bothered if I'd known you'd do something as half-witted as that insurance scheme. What a crazy risk—and for only a few hundred dollars."

"I can't help it about a stupid storm. I intended to put the money back and reactivate the policy as soon as I got some money. No one could live on the chicken feed the bank paid me."

"If he wasn't my friend, I never could have saved you." Buzzy's voice now sounded like a hiss. "I convinced him that the insurance fiasco you caused was the only thing you've ever pulled on your own, that you were young and ambitious. He doesn't know about all your other stunts. He gave you another chance because of me—because of *me*! And I had to foot the bill for all those house repairs the insurance should have paid."

"What did he contact you for, anyway? What's he want now?"

"He only wants you to help clean up this mess by keeping an eye on the girl. He wants to make sure she won't meddle further. If she doesn't cause any more trouble, everything will blow over. That's what we all want. The bank can't tolerate even the smallest type of investigation right now."

"If I can't get decent pay, I'm going it on my own," snapped Johnny.

"Do you think he'd let you do that now? With what you know? Follow orders and stay alive. You need money? Come to me for it. Don't I always give you what you want? But you can't flaunt it. You got to keep a low profile for a while."

Katherine had grown dizzy and wet with sweat from her tight confinement against the plastic bag. The air became more difficult to breathe—warm, stale air with little oxygen left in it. Her lungs felt ready to burst. She could tell that the two men stood close to the barrel. One of them actually brushed against it. If they could hear her as clearly as she heard them, she feared they might hear her gulping breaths.

"I want my own money, and I need my car. I'm tired of driving that rattletrap," Johnny complained.

"Give it a couple more months to make sure nothing comes up about your other deal. Now help me pull this out from the wall. I need you to get this stuff over to the cabin. They shouldn't have brought it here, but I guess they had no choice at the time. Whatever you do, make sure no one sees you."

The shooting pain in her legs grew unbearable. Katherine bit her lip and pressed her head tight against her knees. A scraping sound, accompanied by a tremble in the floor, convinced her they had moved the refrigerator. Silence followed—a deathly kind of silence that she could feel all through her being. She tried to plan for any new emergency. The thought came to her that the vacuum still sat out in the main office. If only they wouldn't notice it.

The silence became torture. She grew more light-headed, but fought it with all her will. The surest way to die would be to faint. If they didn't leave quickly, she would have to jump out. But could she? She wasn't sure she had strength enough to jump anywhere—and she had no weapon but a purse.

Oh God, she prayed, *make them leave now, make them leave now!*

It seemed like an eternity before she heard the sliding sound again, followed by Buzzy's voice.

"Keep an eye on the girl, but don't sneak round. Act friendly with her. If she says anything about the bank problem, let me know. But she won't. I'm sure she's lost interest in the whole matter now that she's down here, and they're repairing her friend's house."

Katherine wanted to scream. Her lungs dug deeper and deeper for the illusive oxygen, but could find none. She felt herself drifting off...drifting ...drifting... an ethereal buzz brought her back. It seemed a lifetime's wait for the second buzz. When it finally came, it sounded distant—like in a dream.

She couldn't wait another second to ascertain they had both gone. With no strength left to climb out or to push the lid off, she thrust her body against the inside of the barrel to upset it, and as she and the container toppled to the floor, she pushed off the lid with her head. She gasped for the fresh air that had been so close, yet so far.

Circulation returned painfully as she tried to stand. Wobbly and bent, she stumbled to the window in time to see the two cars leave the parking lot. It had grown lighter outside, but the world still looked asleep.

She had to get out quickly. The vacuum would have to stay where it sat. Hopefully, whoever found it would think she had forgotten to put it away. Nothing should look different from how it looked right then. She knew she would never clean that office again, but could she even risk working for Buzzy after what she had just overheard? An ominous thought came—*could she risk quitting?*

Prickles went up her spine as she slid through the back door and ran for home. She couldn't help furtively looking over her shoulder for possible pursuers. She crossed the street beside the office, plunged into a tree-lined alley, and nearly collided with a green Jeep parked off the roadside. Bewildered, she looked up, and there in the drivers seat sat the man from the beach.

7

Although the sudden sight gave Katherine a terrible scare, he looked unruffled at her bursting upon him unannounced. Instantly the thought came that he might be a cohort of the Amanos. Had he been watching her? Had he seen her come from the office? The expression on his face baffled her—such a scornful, withering look.

Why? She hurried around the Jeep and ran the rest of the way to her house. She half expected him to give chase, but no one followed her. She rushed inside, locked the door, and sank to the floor. Whom could she trust? What could she do? From their own lips, she learned the worst about Buzzy and Johnny, but how did the Jeep man fit into all of this?

Maybe he sat there in his Jeep for some other reason, and wondered why I ran like some thief or guilty person. Maybe he saw me come out of the office right after the Amano cars left. He would have had a clear view of the office from where he parked. Her face burnt at the thought of how suspicious she would have looked to an innocent bystander.

Katherine reviewed the conversation she had overheard. Both Amanos had made incriminating statements, but they gave only vague details of their crimes—crimes of murder and money. It sounded like a big operation whose tainted claws reached all the way to Chicago, but she had no concrete evidence or information she could give to the police. The police might believe her, but they couldn't arrest anyone on her nebulous statements, and she would end up in worse danger.

For a while she considered giving up everything—her boat, her plans, her Florida. She had stepped into the middle of something terrible. If the Jeep man worked with the Amanos, that put her life in immediate and grave danger. She wanted to believe he didn't. Surely this unknown Chicago person, who gave orders to the Amanos regarding criminal affairs, wouldn't tell both this man and Johnny to watch her.

She would have to investigate the Jeep man further to see how he fit into all of this. In the meantime, her life depended on how well she could appear natural around Buzzy and Johnny. She mustn't arouse their suspicions. They mustn't see any change in her, and she must definitely avoid any mention of Chicago or the bank scheme.

"It *was* a scheme," she said aloud, "Johnny's personal scheme." She knew then that she would have to live with this dreadful shadow hanging over her life until she could learn more.

Lord, I need your help more desperately than I have ever needed it before. I believe you want me to stay here, enjoy the wonderful friends and gifts you have set before me, and wait for your help and guidance. I know I shouldn't turn my back to this terrible situation or run away and allow these crimes to continue, so I will boldly travel the path in front of me until you send me in another direction.

A deep calmness steadied Katherine as she changed to her boating clothes for her final lesson on the *Miss Iris*. She hadn't done anything to the *Miss Iris* yet except to pump its bilge dry once. It still seemed like it belonged to Captain Dale. This trip would officially mark the transfer of ownership to her mind's satisfaction.

The captain met her at the boat and seemed to realize exactly what she most needed to learn. He explained about the engine's care and the equipment.

"Now take her in and out of the slip a few times," he directed, and took a seat beside her.

After some decidedly sloppy docking attempts, he told Katherine to head out into the main channel towards Gordon Pass and the Gulf of Mexico. All along the way, when opportunity arose, he let her try the depth finder and other instruments while he instructed her about shallow areas, sandbars, and inclement weather. Upon reaching the Gulf, they trolled near the shoreline while he explained marine traffic rules to her. Before she had quite assimilated that information, he went on to the subjects of night boating, horn blasts, lights, and charts.

Her head began to swim in spite of all the notes she took. He kept her too busy to even think about her early morning fright, though fleeting visions of the garbage barrel sent chills through her at times.

"Let's fish." he called from one of the fishing chairs. "I'm your first party. Now show me some good places to find them."

All the rest of the day, she operated the boat while he fished. They caught enough to make the day a success.

"You'll want to study navigation somewhere before you get your guide boat captain's license," he said after she had docked the boat. "There's more to learn than I've taught you. Sometime, we'll take her out at night so you can see what I meant about the lights—how the color you're seein' will tell you about the boat you can't see. Night navigation's a whole different story...now grab your half of the fish."

"I can't use but one. You take all of them this time."

"I'll run them down to the fish house then—if you're sure."

She helped him load the catch into his vehicle, and after he left, she hosed down the *Miss Iris* and looked over its possibilities with the eyes of a new owner. With some hastily formed plans for improvement, she headed home, stopping at Captain Dale's house on the way to return a thermos he had left aboard the boat.

Iris worked in the yard. "Miss Katherine, ya just missed Dale."

"I came to return his thermos and to thank you for the jelly. I love it—I've never had that kind before. Also, I came to see if you'd like to go to the Sunday morning service with me."

"Oh, I don't know as I could go tomorrow," Iris hesitated, and then asked, "Would ya like to come in for some tea, though?"

"I'd love to."

Iris scurried around the kitchen as if excited to have a guest. Before joining Katherine at the table, she removed her apron and secured a stray ringlet of silver-gray hair that had escaped the tight braid encircling her head. Though somewhat out of date in her long, shapeless dresses, she always looked tidy. The old-fashioned house looked neat and clean too, with knickknacks covering the walls and every available surface.

"You have such beautiful shells. I never see any of these on the beach."

"You won't find a whole lotta shells around anymore. Most all of these come from Marco."

"Marco Island? I wouldn't think you could find any shells there. I thought condominiums had taken over the island."

"Not back when I was a kid. Marco was just a tiny fishin' village. My daddy fished, and most of the boys took to fishin' when they grew up."

"Did you have a big family?"

"Seven of us kids, and nary a one of us had ever seen a condominium—but there was tons of shells on the beach in them days. Here, I'll show ya some of them." Iris brought out a large box containing bags of shells. "I haven't been into them for a spell."

"Did you gather all of these when you were a child?"

"I've collected all my life. I found some here on the Naples beach, and Dale used to bring home shells when he found a nice or unusual one."

By the time they had gone through the fourth bag of shells, Iris looked up thoughtfully.

"Ya know, I might can go with ya just to the mornin' church service."

"Wonderful," responded Katherine. "Everyone's friendly there, but I still feel uncomfortable going alone."

"Yes'm, they was always a right friendly bunch. I went there a long time ago." Iris seemed closemouthed about many things, so rather than ask questions, Katherine respected her privacy.

Later, as Katherine drove home, she began to relive that morning's terrifying incident. All day she had been around people and had put it out of her mind, but now she was alone. She realized she would be even more alone when she reached her little house that sat much too close to the real estate office. Real panic assailed her when she parked her car and entered the dark interior.

A quick study of its rooms convinced her no one had been there during her absence, but before going to bed, she locked the doors and closed all the windows. Sleep remained elusive as her wide-awake imagination read peril into every shadow and sound. At length, sunlight heralded a new day and a chance to stay in more populated places.

She parked at Iris's house, and they walked the short distance to church.

Many people in the church knew Iris. The woman responded warmly to the numerous welcomes and hugs she received. Although she said little, her face and eyes shone.

They finally found seats near the back.

Katherine looked around and discovered the Jeep man standing at the back of the church talking with two older men. He wore a gray suit, and something about him jogged distant memories of a place where Jeeps and beaches didn't belong. The feeling vanished, but she continued to observe him until she ascertained he was a regular parishioner of this church. He wasn't here to spy, and her inner alarm powered down. After the service, she searched the room, but couldn't see him anywhere. Relieved, she turned back to Iris.

"That was right nice. I reckon I'd like to go again next Sunday." Iris glowed with happiness.

"I'm glad you liked it. I think I have next weekend off, but sometimes I have to work Sunday afternoon. If they called me in, I'd have to leave the service early."

"Leave whenever ya have to. I may just hang

around a spell to catch up on news. I haven't been out much, lately."

They said goodbye at Iris's house, and Katherine drove to her boat. She had packed a lunch that morning so she could stay for a while. She preferred a public place where no one could catch her alone again, and the boat docks stayed busy on a weekend. After she had settled onto a fishing chair and eaten her lunch, she realized she still looked forward to fixing up the boat, even after her earthshaking experience. The sea air seemed to blow away fears and troubles. She decided to begin the job on Monday after work.

Examining the boat for ideas, she came upon a couple of rods and some tackle that Captain Dale had left with the boat. Choosing one of the lighter rods, she stood on the boat's bow and practiced casts for a while.

I'm much better. I'll try it on the beach Monday and dare Mr. Green Jeep to make fun of me—if he comes, that is.

After she tired of that pursuit, she settled back into one of the boat chairs and read until early evening. When she got into her car to leave, she spotted Johnny's blue sedan. Her terror returned with frightful intensity, and she heard Buzzy's words again—*no more killing, Johnny.* While he slowly circled the parking lot, she sat petrified, her hands frozen to her steering wheel. She had tried to forget it actually happened, but Johnny's presence served as an ominous reminder, and now he knew her boat's location.

He's watching me. This probably isn't his first time to drive by.

It was inevitable he'd find out about the boat. Aware that she must barricade her feelings behind a casual, unsuspecting attitude, she forced a smile and wave as he drove past.

He slacked his speed as if he intended to stop, evidently thought better of it, and leaned out his window to wave as he drove on.

"Whew! So far so good," she said out loud in breathless relief, but she still waited a half an hour before she left for home.

The sun already tinged golden highlights across the water when she pulled into an empty parking spot beside the green Jeep the next morning.

Perfect.

Katherine grabbed rod and tackle, and marched the way any accomplished boat captain should. With red shorts, a red-and-white striped sun top, and new casting experience, she prepared to flaunt all her skills. "Good morning," she said pleasantly as she passed him and proceeded down the beach.

When she found a satisfactory spot, she waded in and began to cast her lure into the surf. She didn't accomplish much distance, but no backlashes or rogue fishhooks marred her performance. The saltwater stung the slowly healing wound on her thigh, but she gritted her teeth and continued her little show.

For about fifteen minutes, all went well as she showed off for anyone who might bother to watch. If only some large fish would strike, that would be perfect. With her concentration completely settled on the job at hand, the terrifically painful stab that penetrated the arch of her right foot took her totally by surprise. She looked down, but could see nothing in the stirred up surf and sand around her feet.

Pain grew move severe by the second. She hobbled to shore and upon examination found a dark hole in her flesh. She scooped up her fishing gear and limped back towards the car. Halfway there, she noticed that

Green Jeep had turned his full attention towards her pathetic exit. With effort, she straightened her body and tried to walk normal—but too late.

He came towards her. "What this time?" he demanded in mock annoyance. "Another fishhook?" In spite of his impertinent question, she saw genuine concern in his eyes.

"I think I've been *stabbed* by something." She tried to reply cheerfully, but levity deserted when she heard the tremble of pain in her voice.

The concern in his eyes quickly turned to sympathy.

She stared into those hazel eyes and decided they looked warm, a warm hazel...

"Show me the place."

Jerked from her thoughts, she sat down on the wet sand and showed him the dark hole in her foot. "How can such a tiny wound hurt so terribly?"

"Because of the poison. A school of stingrays just passed me. One of them must have barbed you. Looks like a good sized hole, probably deep." He examined the puncture.

"Ouch," she exclaimed. "I'm sorry. I'm not usually such a baby about pain, but I do sometimes have extreme reactions to poisons—wasps, bees, things like that."

"A doctor once told me that the pain from a stingray stab compared to the pain of a heart attack in intensity. This looks like a bad one."

Her leg had turned a mottled red-and-white all the way up to her knee. She dug fingers tightly into palms to fight the pain now throbbing up her entire leg.

"May I drive you to a doctor? Do you have a doctor?"

"Not yet. I haven't lived here for long," she said as he helped her to her feet.

She avoided his further help, took her rod and tackle, and limped up the beach to her car. By the time she reached it, the ache had heightened unbearably. She stood by her car door and held her keys helplessly, waiting for the pain to ease.

"May I drive you?" he offered again, gently. "I'm Lee Thorpe. I have a business here. People know me." He took the keys from her hand, locked her fishing gear in her car, and handed her the purse he found on the front seat.

For a second, she thought about his presence in the alley on that terrible morning, but then she had also seen him at church. Pain was crowding out everything else, and in desperation she welcomed his aid into the Jeep.

At a doctor's office, he helped her to a waiting room chair. She gripped the wooden armrests fiercely. Her entire leg had turned a dull red.

Lee tried to make conversation, but soon realized pain had taken her beyond that.

A nurse came into the waiting room. "We realize you're in agony," she said. "Please follow me."

Lee accompanied her into the examination room.

The doctor promptly gave her a shot in her injured foot. "You have a deep wound here. The Novocain should take care of the pain," he assured her as he probed for barb remnants. "You should already notice a difference."

"The same Novocain that dentists use?" she asked

"Same thing."

"What do I do when it wears off?"

"Probably nothing. We've discovered that with

stingray wounds, as soon as the Novocain wears off, the pain has usually left also. You should treat it like any other puncture wound. The wound itself may hurt somewhat. I want you to soak it with hot Epsom salts and elevate your foot as much as possible."

When the doctor had finished, Lee helped her out to the Jeep and drove her home. He didn't ask the way, and she reflected that he must have taken note of it that Saturday morning—that perilous Saturday she wanted to forget.

"You should sleep for a while," he said after he had helped her inside. "When you wake up, it'll feel much better, and you can soak it. I'll get your car."

She started to get her car keys but realized he had never returned them.

"Thank you for helping me," she said, as he went out the door.

He smiled his goodbye.

Two hours later, she awoke to a soft tap on her door.

"Your car's in your drive and locked." He handed her the keys. "How does your foot feel?"

"Perfect. Well, almost perfect. Good enough to go to work."

"You'll regret it."

"I've never been stung by a stingray before. If I stay here, I'll miss all the sympathy I'm going to get."

"I knew you did it for sympathy," he said, grinning. "That's why I didn't fall for it. Any girl who would deliberately hook herself with a fishhook is capable of trying anything for attention."

She noted his tongue-in-cheek expression and laughed.

"Really, you'll wish you'd stayed off your foot by

the time you get home today. I know. I've been hit by rays before. Did you ever see a grown man cry?"

She looked at him dubiously and noticed the mischief in his eyes.

"I can't miss work today. I've already made plans for my day off this week, and I don't want to lose it."

"Remember I warned you," he said as he started to leave. He leaned towards her and looked straight into her eyes. "You leave too much slack, and you don't use enough weight."

"I-I what?" she stammered, taken aback.

"You leave too much slack line and not enough sinkers," He repeated.

Mischief glistened in his eyes, and she knew he was poking fun at her casting. She slammed the door and couldn't help laughing again.

8

More than once during the remainder of the day, she wished she had listened to Lee and stayed in bed. With the torture of work finally over, she grabbed her briefcase and headed home, but she didn't expect to find Lee parked in her driveway. Before she could turn off her ignition, he had her door open and his arm out for support. He laughed when he saw the high heels on the seat beside her.

"Bad day?" His innocent expression said much.

"Long day." she grimaced as she gingerly stepped out, shoes in hand.

He helped her into the house and into a soft chair. It took him only seconds to find a box and pillow to place strategically in front of her. He lifted her injured foot onto it and went back to his Jeep for the largest box of Epsom salts she had ever seen.

She started to rise, but he placed his hand on her shoulder.

"You stay here, Kate—this is my department."

So he had taken it upon himself to name her.

"Kate?" she asked, bemused.

"On your key chain—Kate Gale."

"*Katherine* Gale. Katherine wouldn't fit on, so I had to settle for Kate."

"You'll have to settle for it again because Katherine is too long for me, too. Besides, I already know you now as Kate."

He walked into the kitchen, and she could hear him opening cupboard doors and rummaging. She sank back into the chair and decided she liked this man. Surely he wouldn't engage in Amano type activities. Someday, if she had a chance to know him better, she would ask him why he had parked in that alley.

When only an extended silence came from the kitchen, she hobbled out to see if he needed help. She found him looking down at something by her telephone. He hadn't heard her approach because he turned sharply when he saw her.

"It's about ready. I'll be right in."

When he finally returned with a pan of hot Epson salt water, he wore a frown, and his friendly manner had all but vanished. Brisk and businesslike, he submerged her foot into the water.

"Oh! Too hot." She jerked it out.

"Keep plunging it in until you can keep it submerged, and when the water cools, reheat it and soak your foot some more. I have to go, now."

He was out the door before she could thank him. Stung by his sudden personality change, she wondered what upset him.

An hour in the Epson salts took away most of the soreness. Restless and unsettled, Katherine decided to work for a while on her boat. Restless and unsettled, she loaded cleaning supplies and tools, even bedclothes, into her car and headed to the marina.

By the time she arrived, it had grown dark out. She plugged the boat into the dock's electric and turned on the only light in the cabin, a bulb hanging from the ceiling. The cabin had always looked depressing, but now it looked even worse with that bare bulb exposing all its shortcomings and a lifetime's accumulation of dirt. Apparently, no one had ever attempted to clean or improve the cabin's appearance. It had served as a place to stow fishing gear and the other paraphernalia of the fishing business.

Katherine tried to remember how that other cabin looked, the one she toured on her first Sunday in Naples, and made plans as she scrubbed away at the grimy surfaces. The tedious work progressed slowly in spite of the small area. When she finished, she discovered the cabin surfaces wouldn't need further attention. The light gray walls and floor looked freshly painted.

Right away, she saw other possibilities for improvement. She would have to discard a few items and buy a few things, but she would enjoy that part of the job. The tiny galley intrigued her most. That area had taken the longest to clean, but now she could hardly wait to buy kitchenware and fix her first meal there.

"Fish. I'll cook fish," she told the shiny stove.

For a wistful second she thought of how she would like to invite Lee over to share that first meal, and then promptly stopped such a thought.

Weary from her ultra long day, Katherine decided to spend the rest of the night aboard. She felt tired enough to sleep anywhere, but the low-built, storage-box bed immediately made known its inadequacies. She could actually rest her hand on the floor while lying prone, and the inch-thick, plastic covered mattress didn't sufficiently mask the unforgiving qualities of the wood.

"Tomorrow I'll buy foam." She groaned and tried

to get comfortable. Before long, the awe of her presence there in the boat outweighed her discomfort. She listened to the gentle lap of the water, and her thoughts soon turned to Lee. He interested her immensely, but Katherine couldn't understand his mercurial personality. Half asleep, her thoughts drifted waywardly. *Sometimes he seems...nice...*

In the middle of the night, she awoke, confused. Mentally she traveled from the Chicago apartment, to her car, and finally, to the Florida house. In her state of grogginess, nothing fit. She reached a hand off the side of her bed and touched the cool, wet floor.

"The pump! I forgot it!"

When she rushed to turn on the bilge pump, she slipped on the wet cabin floor and banged her head hard against unfamiliar surroundings. With pounding heart, she recovered her balance and located the switch Captain Dale had shown her. Probably four or five days had passed since she last pumped it. When the pump had drained the bilge, she crawled back onto the hard bed, nursing her new hurts. After that, she checked for water every few minutes. Finally, with one hand resting on the floor, she fell asleep.

Morning came and she hurried back to the house to get breakfast and dress for work. When she straightened the kitchen counter, she noticed that her copy of the bank clipping sat there in full view by the phone. She had left it there after her talk with Laura. Was that what Lee studied when she caught him unawares? Did it mean he was involved with the Amanos, and, like Johnny, watched her?

Surely I'm not threat enough for two people to watch me. I'm down here now, and I haven't any reason to cause them further trouble.

Lee had seen her furtive departure from the office that morning. If he was caught up in the Amanos' dealings, if he had told them where and when he saw her, they would realize what she overheard. An icy chill traveled over her body. She tried to think more rationally. Probably Lee hadn't looked at the bank picture. Maybe he happened to glance down just when she walked into the room. She folded the picture and stuffed it into the bottom of her purse.

It was Tuesday now. If Lee was involved, he would already have told Buzzy and Johnny about Saturday morning. Since Johnny didn't act suspicious when he saw her at the docks on Sunday, she felt certain that neither he nor Buzzy knew of her presence in the office that morning. She could risk going to work, though it would be a trial just to step through the office door.

Katherine pushed her thoughts into happier channels and remembered she had something special awaiting her that night after work. A local store, *Marine World*, advertised that they gave lessons on diving, underwater photography, boating, and navigation. When she asked about the boating-navigation course, she found that they held the class at their Ft. Myers store, meeting every Tuesday at seven o'clock. She immediately signed up for it.

A remnant of soreness decided her to skip the beach. She needed the extra time to dress, anyway. There would be no time to go home and change after work, so she would need attire that could double for work and an evening out—something a little special since she planned to take in a movie or go out to dinner after the class. This would be her first night to go anywhere since her arrival in Florida, and she felt like celebrating.

She chose a thin, aqua colored dress, an old favorite. When she added the earrings that she always wore with it—tiny drops of crystal that hung at the end of short, gold threads—she was pleased with the image in the mirror. The dress complimented her new suntan, and the almost invisible earrings that peeked in and out of her dark hair flashed all the hues of the sea.

At the office, Johnny's and Buzzy's cars were both there.

Even with all her resolve to act natural, Katherine couldn't subdue a shiver as she opened the office door. Her entrance instantly attracted the attention of both men. Their obvious approval of her appearance disgusted her and at the same time heartened her. They didn't seem suspicious. She could generally read people, well, everyone but Lee.

The vacuum she'd left out was gone. Not emotionally ready to step into the kitchen, she went straight to her desk without her usual cup of coffee.

With difficulty, she kept her mind on her work. By eleven o'clock she had formulated a plan to free her permanently from the office-cleaning job. She tapped at Buzzy's half-open door.

"Do you have a minute?"

"Certainly...certainly," he said effusively and smiled. "Come in. Sit down."

She didn't intend to sit down, not while he blatantly leered at her, so she started right in on her speech.

"I had problems cleaning the office. I have allergies, especially dust allergies. This last time I had to leave before I'd finished everything. It hasn't been thoroughly cleaned, so please don't pay me for the extra hour."

"Oh, that explains why Janet found the vacuum out yesterday. I'm sorry, Miss Katherine. We'll have to make other arrangements."

"If you'd like, I can at least clean the kitchen during my day in the office. That shouldn't bother my allergies."

"Don't worry about it, my dear." He ogled her shapely legs, stepped close, and took her unwilling hand. "You're working out well here."

"Thank you," she said as she stepped back into the open doorway and removed her hand.

She had hardly reached the refuge of her desk when Johnny sauntered over. Until that moment, she hadn't realized the immensity of his stature.

"Some getup—too nice for this dingy old office. Who'd have thought a girl as pretty as you would like fishing and boats?"

His uninhibited gaze was disconcerting, but instinct assured her this was not a suspicious Johnny, and logic told her he had watched her other times. How else would he know that she fished? Yes, he would watch her, but not because of someone's instructions. He watched because there was nothing subtle about Johnny. She acted moderately friendly, but kept up her wall of reserve.

"I do love to fish, but it's difficult to find time. I've been so busy lately," she added, anticipating the possibility he might ask her out. She turned to her telephone. Lacking encouragement, Johnny wandered off.

At the close of the day, she had to type the inevitable last-minute contracts and got a late start to her class. Students still entered the store when she arrived, and she hurried into the room with renewed excitement. Here she could associate with people of similar interests and prepare for her captain's license at the same time.

She gaped in astonishment when Lee walked into the room. Why had he come to the class? Her heart beat faster, and she could feel the color in her cheeks. Suspicious that he had followed her, she was surprised when he turned out to be the instructor. He hadn't seen her, so she settled back to study him and not feel self-conscious about it.

He wore loose fitting khakis and a day's growth of whiskers that gave his tan a deeper tint than usual. His almost-black hair curled slightly—as if it had just dried in the breeze. Suddenly he saw her and his piercing gaze challenged her so personally that she looked down and began to doodle on her note pages.

At the culmination of the class, she rose quickly. Under no circumstance did she want him to think she had come to the class because of him.

"Kate."

She recognized his voice and hesitated.

"Wait a minute, Kate," he called again, with laughter in his voice.

She couldn't be rude, not after he had rescued her twice. She waited.

When he finished answering the other student's questions, he walked over and picked up her notebook before she realized his intent. "Let's see what you've learned," he taunted and opened her notes. "Oh, no. Was I that boring?"

Chagrined at her marked up pages, she jerked the notebook out of his grasp. She looked down at the notes and laughed in spite of herself.

"By the way," he continued, "excuse my asking — it's none of my business — but why a boating class?"

"I excuse your asking. It is none of your business. And I own a boat."

That seemed to surprise him as much as it delighted her.

"What kind of boat? Speedboat? Sailboat? Ship?"

"Cabin cruiser."

That left him thoughtful for a second. He examined her through squinted eyes. "Come to dinner with me. We'll talk about your boat."

"I'd like that very much." Once outside, Katherine grew apprehensive. Though she thought she had adequately established Lee's innocence, she kept hearing Buzzy and Johnny's ominous, early-morning conversation. She wondered if she would ever again feel safe alone with someone. "I'll follow you — wherever. That way you won't have to bring me back to my car," she suggested and hoped she sounded natural.

He looked at her dubiously for just an instant and grinned. "Great idea, let's go."

He drove to a rickety looking restaurant that sat right over the water. After he spoke with the hostess at the counter, he led her to a rustic outside table where he pulled out a chair for her, but remained standing. "If you like seafood, you'll have to sample some of everything so you'll know what to order next time."

She couldn't squelch a slight thrill that he spoke as if they would come there again.

"I like everything. You can't go wrong with me. Besides, I'm starved."

"Coming up," he assured her as he headed towards the kitchen.

The chef evidently knew him well. They talked and laughed together as he mounded two platters with an assortment of seafood.

"Well, for once in my life I'll finally get enough seafood," she said when he placed the overloaded platter on the table.

"If you don't, I'll go back for more."

A server arrived with iced tea and salads.

When they were alone again, Lee looked at her with challenge in his eyes.

"Will you say the blessing, or do I?"

She bowed her head and prayed quietly—"Thank you, Lord, for this food. Amen."

"You're not a person of many words, are you?"

"Don't men find that a virtue in women?" She sampled one of the crab legs. "Um—umm, good. You won't get much talk out of me tonight."

"No talk, no food," he teased, and then became more serious. "Tell me about this boat of yours."

"It's old and made of wood. How long have you taught this boating class? Do you work for the store, or is this something you do on your own?"

"It's my store." He didn't look up, but continued eating.

"I've been to the one in Naples. Is it part of a chain, then?"

"I have eleven. I guess you could call it a chain—a small chain."

Taken aback, she ate in silence for a minute. She felt better about him now that she knew he owned a business, but she also realized that business ownership didn't prove honesty. After all, Buzzy owned a great amount of real estate, and people considered him a reputable businessperson.

"How long have you had this boat?" he asked, breaking into her thoughts.

"About a week." She nibbled a piece of clam and tried to act nonchalant.

"This isn't your first boat, then."

"First boat," she admitted without meeting his eyes.

"How big?"

"Forty feet. It belonged to a charter boat captain— Dale Townsend."

"Captain Townsend's old boat?" Lee choked. He looked at her in amazement. "So that's why you came to my class. That's a lot of boat for one person to handle, especially someone new to boating."

"I've run her a few times with Captain Dale's help. He taught me a lot—and I'm studying every chance I get."

"What would a real estate salesperson want with a boat like that? Do you intend to sell islands to fishermen?" His face showed amusement.

"I hope I won't be involved in real estate sales at all." She would never tell him her plans for the boat, not after his insults of her casting. She could already hear him laughing.

A dark look came over his face, the same one she had witnessed that morning in the alley and again in her kitchen when he fixed the Epsom salts. It unnerved her.

After a while, he seemed to throw off his mood and looked at her thoughtfully. "Would you like a tour in my motor boat? I could introduce you to some of the channels and inland waterways around this area. How about Saturday?"

She started to accept what sounded like a

wonderful prospect. But her caution stepped in with a blinking red light and reminded her of the Amanos. Lee could easily use such a trip to do away with her. It sounded far-fetched, but so did the words she heard from that barrel. She couldn't take the chance, not with anyone, not yet.

"I...can't this weekend." She saw his disappointment and felt her own. "Maybe later. Maybe Thursday or Friday next week. " Maybe by next week she would know more about him.

"Will you come to next Tuesday's class?"

"Certainly."

"Don't eat before you come...would you like more fish? Some dessert? I didn't think you could do it, but you've emptied the platter. That's a first for one of my dates."

"I'm glad I'm a date. The bill for this will be astronomical," she teased. "I believe I will have dessert, but first maybe a few more crab legs—and a dab more of that butter sauce dip."

"I've created a monster, but I'll share some more crab with you while we wait for dessert." When he brought back another sizeable platter of crab legs, she feared she couldn't live up to her boast.

"I've never tasted seafood like this. It has...flavor."

"No wonder. I've noticed your license tag. Where would you get fresh seafood like this way up there? These critters came straight from the water. Where in Illinois did you live?"

"Chicago."

"Why'd you leave? Too cold for you?

"Much too cold, and it was something I'd planned for a long time." She didn't intend to reveal much, especially the car incident in Chicago.

The arrival of their colorful dessert prevented further conversation. Katherine stared in awe at the tall, orange mousse in front of her. Covered with crushed strawberry sauce and topped with whipped cream, it looked too beautiful to eat. "Oh!" she wailed. "I shouldn't have ordered more crab legs, but you..." she pointed an accusing finger at him, "you goaded me on."

"I didn't want you to suffer hunger pains and blame me," he said with a pleased expression.

They both managed to empty their dessert dishes.

"You didn't leave anything for the garbage pail. Are you always that hungry?"

"I don't generally leave food, but I couldn't have eaten one more item tonight."

"Good. I haven't failed you after all."

When they went out to their vehicles, Lee drew a map for her.

"This route's the best way back to Naples from here...by the way, I plan to take this route myself, and I hate the thought of a flat tire late at night with no one around to help change it. Would you follow me—just in case I need aid?"

She laughed at his clever offer of protection and began to trust him. "After you, brave knight," she quipped.

9

Katherine stayed too busy to worry extensively about her precarious situation for the next few days. The move from a house to a small area like a boat turned into a more involved undertaking than she had expected. She skipped her morning walks, and even slept aboard the *Miss Iris* so she could work late on the boat.

She purchased two, ten-inch-thick pieces of foam and twelve yards of navy blue and white print fabric. Although she had a sewing machine at her house and could have worked comfortably there, she preferred to work at her boat without the machine's motor vying with the sounds of lapping water and fish jumping. At night, she sewed by hand a complete set of curtains for all of the small windows. With the remaining portion of the material, she covered the pieces of foam, which became mattresses for the built-in wooden beds.

Amazed at the difference those made in the cabin, Katherine went on another shopping spree the next day and came back laden with interesting packages. She was excited about the transformation she could now clearly visualize.

The first bundle consisted of half a dozen, red and blue pillows, two small bedspreads that matched the decor, two marine wall lamps, a floor-length, unbreakable mirror, blue and red potholders with matching dishtowels, and an inexpensive set of colorful, unbreakable dishes, tumblers, and cups.

After she had placed everything just so, she brought in a deep, soft, navy-blue rug with rubber backing. Measuring and cutting it to size, she spread it over her tiny cabin floor. It stayed in place nicely, yet she could easily take it up and dry it if she ever forgot the bilge pump again. The carpet made the greatest difference in the cabin and officially marked the end of her moving tasks.

She stood in the doorway of the cabin and surveyed the changes. The cabin now looked like a clean, cozy apartment, and she had captured the nautical effect. She wished she could show it to someone.

Finally she brought in her last bundle. She spread its contents out on the two beds and gloated over the rainbow-hued pile of new clothes—uncrushable garments. She hadn't been able to resist the purchase of a fresh look for herself as well as her boat, but she only bought clothes that wouldn't wrinkle when folded and stacked with other garments. She fingered the wonderful fabrics and found it difficult to fold them away and crawl into bed.

When morning arrived, Katherine was tempted to laze around since she didn't have to go to work. But her plans for the day didn't include rest.

It took only minutes to make the bunk back into a sofa, slip into her boating clothes, and prepare for her first solo voyage. Breakfast would have to wait. She wanted to start early so that fewer boaters could observe her novice boatmanship. She tried the ignition and the engine started.

Her heart thumped in excitement. She threw off the mooring lines and steered the *Miss Iris* out of the slip and towards the channel. The engine ran barely above an idle, but it still seemed too fast. When she safely entered the buoy-lined main channel, she sighed in relief.

At trolling speed, she headed down the bay. Everything went smoothly, and she had actually started to enjoy herself when out ahead she saw the pass into open water. She almost panicked. The bay had ended. She had done it all before, the water looked calm, and much smaller boats zoomed around in the Gulf with no trouble.

"Time to go for it, Captain." Katherine headed into the Gulf.

The water looked tranquil and clear—so blue. She could easily make out the shallower areas of sand bars. She was tempted to weigh anchor and just sit there offshore for a while, but she finally opted for more practice.

She circled and headed back into the bay. When she neared her home docks, she circled again and repeated her first trip. The second time she reached home she attempted her first solo docking. It took two tries and some minor bumps, but she accomplished the task.

At that moment, Katherine realized how much she loved the *Miss Iris*. She wanted to clean her, pamper her, and listen to the water lap against the hull. She wanted to smell the salt air and forget Chicago with its noise, traffic, and cold weather. Most of all, she wanted to forget the dead-end feeling she used to have. She was glad she had bought the *Miss Iris*.

She idled away the rest of the day—read for a while and finally fished from the docks. Late in the afternoon, fishing yielded a snapper, which she took into her tiny galley for a celebration supper of her first solo trip.

In the morning, Iris walked with Katherine to church again. Katherine was pleased at Iris's growing hunger for outside associations. Iris had confided in her that she rarely had visitors and that she had hardly left her property during the last twenty years except to buy groceries. Now she attended all the services the church afforded whether Katherine accompanied her or not.

Katherine turned to ask for a hymnal and noticed Lee. He took a seat near the back of the church. By service end, he had disappeared as before, and she wondered where he went.

"I'm so glad the Miss Iris is docked near you and the church," Katherine mentioned on their walk home.

"Ya need to give her a new name when ya paint her. That was a fool thing for Dale to do, namin' her after me."

"The name seems to fit her. I like it."

"Fiddlesticks with that. Name her somethin' that fits ya, something that sounds adventurous."

"You mean like *Miss Adventure?* I definitely don't need a misadventure, right now."

Between work duties and short test runs with the Miss Iris, Tuesday was upon Katherine before she realized it. She dressed in one of her new acquisitions, a violet sundress with straps of tiny roses, in anticipation of her boating class that night. She waited until the last minute to show up for work so that she wouldn't be alone with Buzzy or Johnny. Johnny had become a slight problem, showing up unexpectedly during her off work hours.

Relieved to find only Buzzy to contend with, she

quickly started work and hoped he hadn't taken note of her arrival. Just as she began typing a contract, he walked over.

"You know what, Katherine? That Johnny of mine just put through an impressive deal. When you get your license, I may want you to work with him. You're a hard worker, too, and you two would make a good team—*Kathy and Johnny*. You'd probably become my top selling team." He chuckled as he walked back into his office.

Though he hadn't made any fresh advances, this new fatherly Buzzy revolted her almost as much as the other one. Now he wanted to pair her off with Johnny. In some instances, his pride of his son might be commendable, but she found it nauseating.

She wondered how she would feel if she had a son like Johnny. Could she still love him, knowing the horrendous deeds that he had committed, or was this father guilty of worse crimes?

Lee's reaction to her dress that night more than lived up to her expectations. He said nothing, but took her hand and looked at her until she became embarrassed.

"I think the class just called for their teacher." She laughed self-consciously and pulled her hand away.

Their eyes met often while he taught. She wondered if she had fallen for Lee, or for the glamour of Florida and her new lifestyle. Would Lee seem as attractive to her if they both lived in Chicago? She was deep in thought when a hand tapped her shoulder.

"Wake up. Class dismissed—time to eat."

"My turn to treat. I saw a fast-food establishment just a block away."

He gave her a withering glance. "No chance,

Captain. We have other plans. Do you trust me to drive this week, or do you plan to follow behind again?"

"If you drive like you teach, I'm sure I'll feel safe. Lead on," she quipped.

"Sometimes I'm not sure about you, Kate."

Instead of taking Katherine to a restaurant, he drove to a beach she had never seen before, a lonely stretch of sand at a lonely time of night. Noting a few other cars parked there, she prepared to enjoy herself.

"This is Wiggin's pass. Sometimes I come here at night to fish," he explained as he brought baskets and bags out of the back of his Jeep.

She helped carry them and noted the dark shapes of people fishing at the water's edge. Lee spread a blanket for her and turned on a small battery powered lantern. It gave adequate light for his work without breaking the mood of the place. Within minutes, he had a fire started in a small grill he brought.

"The warmth feels good. I felt chilly until you built the fire."

"People used to build bonfires down here and spend all night on the beach. The authorities frown on that now, but we can make this fire bigger after we're through cooking as long as it doesn't outgrow the grill."

"Oh, will we cook? Do I have to catch the fish we eat?"

"With your casting? We'd starve."

She quickly dug both hands into the white sand, blatantly showing him her evil intent, and he just as precipitously trapped them beneath his own. She saw his split second of hesitation quickly turn to brashness as he leaned forward and kissed her lips.

"My apologies, Ma'am. Am I forgiven?" he

entreated while he still had her hands pinned and harmless.

To hide how shaken his kiss had left her, she purposely pretended to misunderstand why he sought forgiveness.

"Sir, I had snapper for supper last night, in spite of my poor casting. What did you have?"

"Hamburger—slightly burnt." He released her hands and grinned.

"I guess I came to the wrong place for dinner if that's how you cook."

When she jumped up, he grabbed her hands again.

"Not my fault. The phone rang, and I couldn't get off the line. Besides, you're stranded. No boat, no car—just me."

"I still have my legs."

"Yes…I've noticed that," he bantered with half-comical, half-meaningful glance.

"You're standing on dangerous sand."

"Please forgive me. I promise—no more jokes about your casting…tonight, anyway."

She sat back comfortably on the blanket, and he brought out an assortment of seafood. On one side of the grill, he arranged shrimp, fish, oysters on the half-shell, and two lobster tails. On the other side, he set a small, blackened saucepan, which he filled with water.

He left and returned with a piece of green stick, which he placed across the top of the pan.

"Excuse me—but what sort of brew are you concocting in that little pan?"

"Heating water for tea or coffee. The stick keeps it from boiling over—usually. Don't ask how." He took a minute to move some of the seafood towards the cooler edges of the grill before returning his attention to

Katherine.

"Does your family live in Illinois or Florida?"

"Neither. My father died when I was twelve, and my mother lives in New York. What about *your* family?"

"Both of my parents have passed on."

"I'm sorry...any other family?"

"I had an aunt, my best buddy, but I lost her recently. Coffee or tea ma'am?" he changed the subject.

"It seems like a coffee night."

"Coffee it is, then."

He poured some grounds into the boiling water and served the seafood. While they ate, he bombarded her with a seemingly endless supply of questions: What did she do in Chicago? How long had she done it? With what office? Why did she leave? How did she get the job with Buzzy Amano? Why did she buy the *Miss Iris*?

She answered as honestly as possible, but avoided any mention of Laura's bank problem or of her terrifying car incident in Chicago.

"So you quit your job, secured another one over the phone, and moved the next day. If you'd considered this move for years, why the sudden haste?"

"Haven't you ever just reached the point where enough is enough? I was ready, and I did it—the same way I bought the boat," she snapped at him and put down her plate in exasperation.

"You mean she who hesitates is lost?"

"Exactly." The words no sooner left her mouth than she realized she had fallen right into his trap. She was suddenly wrapped close in strong arms, a rough cheek pressed hard against hers, and his lips close by her ear.

"Like this you mean?" he asked huskily, kissed her shoulder, her neck, and ultimately found her lips that parted in shock.

For a minute, she allowed herself the warmth of his closeness. She could feel his strong heartbeat through his soft flannel shirt, and then it seemed as if it was *her* heartbeat. She freed one arm and gently pushed him away, but his warmth lingered with her as they sat for a while in silence.

"Let's walk," he suggested, and reached for her hand.

Her fear totally gone, she strolled with him down the beach. The surf rolling around their feet felt warmer than she had expected. In the four weeks since she'd moved there, the temperature had warmed, especially during the last week.

"I see gray shadows crossing back and forth on the beach. Is it an illusion?" she asked and broke the silence.

"Ghost crabs. You have to be quick to catch one."

They chased and laughed until they had scared all the crabs into holes. When they returned to the dying coals of their fire, Lee lay back on the blanket with his hands behind his head. For the longest time he said nothing. Although she looked out to sea, she could feel his penetrating eyes. She finally turned and met his gaze.

"Will you come here with me again? We could fish, and eat. The later it gets, the nicer it gets. Will you come?" he asked again wistfully.

"I love the ocean at night. I once spent almost an entire night on the pier. Remember that morning you caught me napping in my car?"

"I'll consider it a date, then. We'll pick a night when you don't have to work the next day."

"I'd love that, and *I'll* bring the picnic next time."

A feeling of awe and sweet companionship lingered with Katherine as they reluctantly packed to go. Had something real happened, or had the enchantment of the place seduced her feelings. Whatever had happened, he seemed to feel it, too.

He wouldn't let her drive the thirty miles back to Naples unescorted, so the green Jeep accompanied her all the way to her marina. And, of course, since he was already there, she couldn't resist showing him her newly decorated cabin.

"It makes me think of you," he commented after a careful examination of everything she had done.

"Me?"

"It's soft," he said and squeezed one of the new pillows, "and it's neat. It smells good. It contains much more than meets the eye...it's beautiful, it's..." he rested his hands firmly on her shoulders, "warm."

"It's late," she whispered and caught her breath.

10

It felt good to awake the next morning full of excitement and anticipation. No lingering doubts about Lee troubled her, and her fear of Buzzy and Johnny had diminished overnight. She had a friend now, and sometime soon, she would tell him about her situation.

When she arrived at the beach for her morning walk, she had to stifle her disappointment. Lee never showed up, and when Thursday morning rolled around with still no sign of Lee, her spirits took a nosedive. She had hoped their special outing in his boat would fall on one of her days off. Now she had Thursday and Friday free and no definite plans.

At length, she decided to take her boat out and practice for a while. Just as she prepared to leave the beach, her phone rang. Her heart leapt at the thought of Lee, and dropped as quickly when she heard Buzzy's voice.

"Glad I caught you, Katherine. I need your help today if you can find it possible. You'll be well compensated, and I'll make the time up to you later."

"Of course," she said disappointedly. "Did you want me to work at the condos today?"

"Actually Katherine, I had something entirely different in mind. Remember those pictures you took for me the other day? The Golden Gate ones? Well, we have some new properties on Marco Island—a large condominium complex just completed. I need you to use the office camera and take some pictures for a brochure."

"Of course. I'll—

"I want a slightly different approach this time," he interrupted. "You see, Johnny's told me about your boat. If you're agreeable, the office may need your boating services from time to time. I'd like some offshore pictures of the complex and of the gulf shoreline between Marco and Naples. Maybe get some bay shots, too. This condo complex will be popular with boaters since it will offer nearby, private boat dockage to occupants who own larger boats."

"It sounds great, but I—"

"While you're at the island itself, I want you to take a good selection of pictures, inside and outside shots. Also, photograph some of the nearby places that might interest buyers. You know what I mean—shopping, restaurants, that sort of thing."

"Mr. Amano, I'm a beginner at boating. I haven't gone out by myself except for a few times, and then, not far. I would love to do this job for you, but I don't think I'm qualified—yet."

"Don't worry about a thing, Miss Katherine. It will be a calm day. I've made the same trip many times in my small boat, and I'll give you detailed instructions. I'll write down all the landmarks and show you exactly where to dock. You'll receive double pay for the day, plus gas and expenses. I hope you can do this for us, Katherine, because I definitely see more need of your services in this line and more opportunities for you to earn some good bonuses. We plan to take many of our prospective buyers over to view this property by means of a boat trip. A fishing boat like yours would give the exact atmosphere we'd like to create, and it would hold more people and be more comfortable than a speed boat."

Katherine agreed and made a quick stop at the office for the camera and the map he had drawn for her. Although the route looked clear and detailed, she still felt the need for more assurance. She stopped at Captain Dale's house on the way home, but was disappointed to find him gone.

"I have to take some offshore pictures for my office," she explained to Iris. "I came by for some more advice, but I guess I can handle it."

"Surely ya can. It's a real nice day. Where ya goin'?"

"Marco Island. And there may be more trips later," she added elatedly.

"That's right fine, but I wish ya had someone to go with ya. I know Dale would go if he was here."

"I think I'll be OK."

"Call me when ya get there, and again when ya get back, ya hear me?"

"Yes, I'll call. If you don't hear from me for a day or two, call the Coast Guard," she joked.

"Yes'm, I'll call the Coast Guard if that happens— seein' as it's less'n fifteen miles to Marco," she said with a droll smile.

Once underway, Katherine found everything exactly as Buzzy had noted it. She simply followed the shoreline and stayed out far enough to assure deep water. After passing Kewaydin Island, the spirit of adventure fully captured her. Alone on the open sea, she gloried in the incomparable feeling.

Shortly after passing Isles of Capri, she approached Marco. She hadn't expected such a modern display, or such an overly developed island. With the aid of Buzzy's map, she easily located the condos and the place where he instructed her to tie the *Miss Iris*. A narrow dock extended out into the bay behind the condo buildings.

She pulled near it, and a young man, shirtless and wearing cutoff jeans, came out on the dock towards her. At first, she feared he had come to say she couldn't tie up there, but instead he waved to bring the boat in closer.

"I'm to gas it up for you," he explained pleasantly. "Leave it running and get whatever you need." He held it close to the dock while she climbed out with her purse and camera.

"Look for her right here when you finish your business."

"Do I pay you for the gas now, or when I get back?"

"Your office already took care of that," he said as he jumped aboard.

Katherine concluded that they had built the dock to service the condo. It didn't look like a public docking facility. She saw no stores, gas pumps, or even a hose—only one electric light bulb hanging above it.

She wondered how the young man knew who she was when she hadn't told him anything. Suddenly she laughed at her own naiveté. How many old fishing boats with the name *Miss Iris* painted on them pulled in there? Obviously, Buzzy had called and arranged everything.

With another glance at her instructions, she noted she would be on shore for about three or four hours. Buzzy had told her to take all her offshore pictures on the way back because he preferred sunset shots.

The walk to the complex took only a few minutes.

She photographed everything that looked interesting, including the buildings themselves, which she shot from a number of angles. Inside the main building, she photographed the public areas, the interior of the penthouse model, and some of the other models. She thoroughly enjoyed looking at the exquisitely furnished models. She took a few pictures from the windows, which showed diverse outlooks from different sides of the buildings.

"The view must be fantastic at night," she said enthusiastically to the older salesperson who accompanied her.

"Very impressive. I seldom come here at night, but when I do, I always enjoy looking out at the water and the city lights."

"I'm supposed to go to the Captain's Cabin for dinner and more pictures. Are you familiar with that restaurant? They didn't give me its location."

"It's about two blocks from here. If you can wait five minutes, I'll go with you."

During her leisurely dinner with the semi-retired salesman, she learned much about the Marco area.

"You'll be seeing more of me if Buzzy plans for you to bring clients here regularly. I live on the island and will be working at this complex four days a week. You say you came by boat? It must have been a pleasant trip on a day like this."

"Yes, the Gulf was blue and friendly today. Hopefully, it continues that way until I get back. I have a few more places to photograph before I'm through here."

When Katherine returned to the dock, she found her boat moored exactly as the attendant had promised. She took some pictures from the dock before moving offshore to take shots of the buildings from that angle.

On the way back, she stopped often for pictures and felt satisfied with the collection by the time she reached her marina. She had some beautiful sunset shots and even a few pictures of the *Miss Iris*.

She backed into her slip on the first try and felt more than satisfied with the day when she called Buzzy.

"I have your pictures. Do you want me to bring the camera by the office now?"

"Wonderful, Katherine. I knew I could count on you. Would you hold on to it for now? I want you to have the pictures printed at one of those one-hour photo places. I'll look them over then, and have the brochure made up."

Relieved that she didn't have to meet Buzzy after hours at the office, she downloaded copies of the pictures to her laptop so she could send copies to her mother and Laura and other friends she had neglected.

Finally, she went out to shop and ordered prints of all the photos at a place she found in the back of a department store.

Though elated with her successful boat trip, the threat of the Amanos asserted itself. A responsibility to expose them lay heavy on her mind. She couldn't continue to work for them knowing what she knew, but she also had no solid proof of anything. No matter what direction she took, she must proceed cautiously. Any unusual move on her part might arouse their suspicions.

****

Six days passed with no trace of Lee. When Katherine left for her boating class on Tuesday evening, she began to feel piqued. How should she act when she attended class that night? Maybe she had taken too much for granted—read too much into a kiss. Maybe such a night represented a more common occurrence to him than it did to her.

Common? She couldn't remember ever having a night quite like their date on the beach, but that didn't mean it was an unusual experience with him. There could have been many nights, and many different girls.

By class time, she had built up a shield of reserve. She refused to make a fool of herself. She sat coolly on her cold metal chair, and her heart suddenly took another nosedive as a different instructor walked to the front of the room.

Where was Lee?

Class wasn't the same, but she took notes and listened attentively. She went home disappointed, wondering if Lee had moved on.

Her cell phone interrupted sleep the next morning. With expectations of a call from Lee, she fumbled before managing to hit the correct button.

"Good morning, Miss Katherine—*Captain* Katherine I should say. Did I wake you?" Buzzy's effusive voice echoed in her half-asleep ear. "We need your services as boat captain again today."

"Certainly."

"You won't work at the condos at all today. You'll take two couples and a sales associate, Bill Haines, to Marco. They'll arrive at your boat about one o'clock this afternoon, and you'll receive double pay for an entire day, no matter how quickly you consummate the trip. We'll call it sales pay. Also, if Bill makes a sale because of this trip, you'll receive a bonus. How does that sound to you, Miss Katherine?"

"That sounds fine. Do I take the same route and dock in the same place?"

"I want you to travel to Marco by way of the Intracoastal Waterway and come back by way of the Gulf. That way they'll have a chance to see a little more and still view the sun setting on the water when you return."

"I've never taken the Intracoastal that far before."

"You'll find it easy, safer than the ocean. I'll make a map and have Bill bring it by to you. Gas up in Naples before you leave, and I'll reimburse you."

She couldn't help but applaud Buzzy's plan as she prepared for the day ahead. Who could resist buying one of those gorgeous units after a romantic boat trip through the Florida sunset? Considering what she'd overheard when she hid in the trash can, why did someone like Buzzy, who obviously possessed talent as a businessperson, resort to dishonesty and crime? It made her feel a little sad.

At a nearby marine supply store, she bought ice, bottled drinks, and three light folding chairs especially made for boats. They had pockets in the armrests for drink containers and had large, non-slip tips on the legs, constructed to grip the boat deck. At the checkout counter, she spied some white captain's hats. They tempted her, but she hadn't earned the right, yet. Maybe after she had her guide boat captain's license, she would indulge.

When she dropped by Captain Dale's house for some last minute guidance, he assured her she would have no trouble on the Intracoastal, and he showed her charts on it.

"Stay between the markers and expect slightly stronger current here...and here," he said as he pointed to places on the chart.

When she finished with Dale, she went into the kitchen where Iris worked.

"I'll probably be back in time for church tonight, but don't wait on me if I'm not."

"Come by here and have some dinner with me if you get back early enough. We can walk there together."

The boat trip went well. At Marco, no attendant waited to assist her this time, but Bill moored the boat tightly to the posts and helped his clients disembark. When they started on their walk up to the condos, Katherine loosened the lines and hung her own instant-print camera around her neck. She planned to help Bill any way she could.

They followed somewhat the same schedule she used the day she took pictures. As a group, they toured the complex, and then stopped at the Captain's Cabin for dessert and coffee.

Katherine took pictures of anything that might interest the two couples, and made sure to include the clients in as many shots as she could. She knew it would not only help Bill clinch a sale, but would also give the couples some lasting mementoes of the trip. Although it wasn't a professional camera like the office one, the instant print camera had served well in the same capacity when she sold real estate in Chicago.

The breeze increased on the way back and the water became choppy. She began to understand how quickly conditions could change, and was relieved when she pulled into the slip.

Before everyone said goodbye, she presented the

pictures, which the clients received with more enthusiasm than she had expected, she felt sure Bill would accomplish at least one sale from the day's work.

After a quick cleanup of the boat, Katherine drove to a nearby antique shop and picked up a gift she purchased a few days earlier when she'd shopped for boat accessories. The china cabinet had caught her interest the minute she saw it. The cabinet's unique design made it perfect for Iris's seashell collection, and it would fit nicely in the corner where Iris stored her shell boxes.

When she carried it into Iris's living room, the shining look in the woman's eyes rewarded Katherine tenfold for her efforts.

Iris almost let dinner burn while she placed shells on the many shelves.

After dinner, they still had a few minutes until church time, so they worked on the shells again.

"I'm usin' this spot for my special ones." Iris opened a small box and began placing shells on the most prominent shelf.

"What's this shell that you've given a place of honor?" Katherine picked it up and examined it. "It looks like only a piece of a shell, or is that the way it's made?"

"That's a junonia, and it *is* only a piece of a shell. I've never found a whole one. They're sorta uncommon around here. Someday maybe I'll run across a perfect one and replace this piece."

"I'll write down the name in case I ever see one." Katherine brought out her pen and notebook. "Why don't you give me the names of all the shells, and I'll make labels on my computer."

"Wouldn't that be just fine. 'Cept I don't rightly know who all might see them."

"Maybe you'll invite one of the church ladies over some time."

"I just might at that. The preacher and his wife come by the other day. Dale—he leaves in his boat as soon as he sees them." Iris stared thoughtfully down at her lap for a minute. "We had a real pleasant visit though," she finally added.

"And you'll probably have loads more—especially from me," Katherine said impulsively.

"You're becomin' a regular boat captain, takin' parties out and all. Ya need to get your charter license."

"I know. I've been studying for it. Right now I'm only taking out guests of the office, but if I ever want to charge people for outings, I'll need a license."

"Don't go to takin' men guests out alone on your boat. I mean ones ya don't know. There be some wild ones hereabouts."

"I'm sure of that," Katherine said with a lightness she didn't feel.

"Do ya have a special man friend who can sorta look out for ya? I bet you left some broken hearts back in Chicago."

"No special man anywhere, yet. I haven't dated much recently. I used to date a lot, was even engaged once, but that didn't work out. In that instance, I don't think either of our hearts really broke, though I felt like it at the time."

"Ya look pretty heart healthy to me. Real breaks don't mend that quick or clean. I'm guessing God has saved someone special for ya."

11

Iris's words were still in her mind that evening when Buzzy called again.

"Katherine—more work for you. We've lined up parties for the next three afternoons, and again on Monday. You keep track if you miss any of your days off. Later you can take a vacation when the condo sales slow down. We've had a bigger response to this development than we expected."

"I'm glad my boat helps."

"Helps?" He laughed. "No one wants to *drive* to Marco anymore. We always give them a choice, but they all want a boat ride. Even my associates love the novelty. Both of those parties Bill took out bought condos. One of the ladies showed me the pictures you took for her. Excellent work, Katherine."

Praise from such a man meant little to Katherine, but at least she could gain experience with her boat and still earn her living. Actually, the extra pay had restored much of her depleted savings, and if it continued, she could afford to have work done on the *Miss Iris* soon.

For the next three days, she followed the same procedure. She accompanied the sales associates and their prospects on a tour of the condos, followed by dessert and coffee at the restaurant. The associate generally made a sales pitch at the restaurant, and by the time the buyer or buyers arrived back in home dock with complimentary pictures in hand, the associate could usually consummate a sale.

Katherine understood the power that sun burnished ocean had over people who had just left a raw winter in the north, and most of their buyers did come from northern states. Tired of icy streets and heating bills, most of them came ready to buy.

Monday's party arrived an hour early, and with Johnny as the sales associate.

Katherine froze when she saw him step out of his car, but by the time he boarded the boat, she had her feelings under control. After all, what could happen with four other people aboard?

Johnny motioned her aside when he had his guests situated comfortably. "We're going to pour some extra attention on our guests—give them a tour of Marco and a dinner at the restaurant. We may be gone longer than usual."

At Marco, she was surprised when the young man of her first trip met the boat. He waited, as before, to take the *Miss Iris*.

"It won't need gassed up today," she called pleasantly and stayed at the helm.

"Take these, Billy," Johnny said and threw him the lines.

Upon disembarking, Katherine noticed that Billy had a rod set there at the dock.

"Any luck?" she asked cheerfully.

He seemed confused at first, as if he didn't know what she meant. "Oh, no, nothing today."

"Katherine, take these folks on ahead. I'll catch up in a second," Johnny said.

"Of course." She smiled at his clients. "Follow me."

When she glanced back, she saw Johnny hand something to Billy.

Probably a tip. That's something I didn't think to do.

Johnny caught up and began his sales pitch while she busied herself with picture taking.

It seemed that Johnny took an unnecessarily long time to show the condos. Afterwards, they partook of an unhurried dinner followed by a van tour of Marco. When they finally prepared to board the boat, she looked at her watch and saw this would be her latest trip, so far.

When she stepped into the *Miss Iris*, her foot slipped. Catching her balance, she discovered a small patch of water on the deck. She wiped it dry to prevent anyone else from taking a fall. She didn't remember anyone spilling a drink, and the only other source of nearby water was the very calm Gulf.

She had hardly pulled away from the dock when she noticed something else amiss—her gas gauge read higher than when she docked a few hours earlier. She always checked the gauge when she docked. At first, she reasoned that Johnny had paid Billy to add more gas, but there were no pumps nearby, and she had kept her boat keys. Bearing in mind that the gauge might have malfunctioned, she made a mental note to keep an eye on it until she ascertained its reliability. As she headed towards Naples, the sound of a speedboat drew her attention. Many such boats passed her by on that route, but this one sounded different.

"That's a fast one coming up on our starboard. Wonder what kind of motor it's got," Johnny said admiringly. "A big, old inboard of some kind."

"At least he's keeping a safe distance," Katherine replied. "Some of them cut dangerously close, though their wake seldom bothers a boat this big and sturdy."

She took a second look at the boat as it passed, and suddenly jerked in shock. The operator looked like Lee. Was that possible? She watched him until the boat became a speck in the distance.

Johnny knew about motors, anyway—the boat had incredible speed.

It took a while to convince herself that most of these tanned, shirtless sportsmen looked the same at a distance. Evidently, she saw what she wanted to see, and she wanted to see Lee.

With no more sign of the speedboat, she arrived back in port and tended to boat chores. When she turned on the bilge pump, a ceremony she performed faithfully every evening, it surprised her when only a trickle of water came out. Concerned that her pump had quit working, she opened her hatch and found an almost dry bilge. The pump still worked fine, but she couldn't explain the dryness of the bilge. Leaks didn't fix themselves.

It had certainly been a trip full of irregularities, she thought as she sat back on a deck chair and rested. After much deliberation, she put together a plausible, but not very convincing explanation for everything. She concluded that possibly Johnny didn't trust her seamanship and paid Billy to check over the boat and add more gas from a gas can. Billy could have brought a bottle of water with him and spilled some on the deck.

Katherine gazed, unseeing, as she thought this over. Adjusting her sight, she realized she was staring at a dark smudge by the tiny gutter of a hatch opening. She got down to examine it more closely. It looked like the crushed ashes of a cigarette, and an accumulation filled the gutter. No smokers had come on the boat that day, and she had never seen Billy with a cigarette—though it was possible he smoked. At least the ashes proved that *someone* had boarded the boat during her absence.

She scooped the small accumulation of ash into an envelope and decided from its slightly sweet scent that it probably came from a pipe or a mild cigar. When she opened that hatch and examined the area below it, she found another bit of ash. She lowered her head further in to see if she had missed anything, but the hold contained nothing except a slight tobacco scent, the same sweet scent of the other ashes. For some reason, someone who smoked had opened that hatch and had leaned over it. That was an unsettling thought.

A call from Buzzy ended her investigations for the time being.

"Katherine, we've lined up a trip for tomorrow—the usual short one. Show the condo, buy them dessert, and bring them back. Plan on it starting later since they can't leave until three, but don't worry, you should get back before dark."

"Tuesday is my day in the office. Do you want me to come in and work until boat time?"

"That won't be necessary. You're more valuable to the firm in this capacity. Why, Miss Katherine, we've had Marco residents drive here to Naples so that they can ride your boat back to Marco and view the condos." He laughed at the absurdity.

For the first time, she wished she could forgo the boat trip. She would rather spend a boring day in the office than miss her class that night. Now she would have to wait another week to see Lee—unless she made some kind of record time on her boat trip.

Katherine experienced an agreeable surprise when Alice showed up the next day with two elderly couples. When they arrived in Marco to view the condos, they turned out to be slow lookers. For a short while, Katherine cherished a forlorn hope she might still make the class, but after several unsuccessful attempts to speed everyone up, she finally admitted defeat.

While Alice and her clients enjoyed coffee at the restaurant, Katherine left the table to go to the restroom. It surprised her to see Billy, from the dock, standing in a back hallway. Dressed in a suit, he appeared older. He gave some sort of instructions to one of the waiters, and then disappeared into an office.

When she got back to her table, Alice had an apologetic look on her face.

"While you were gone, all four of our friends here have expressed a desire to look at the condos again. Will we have time for that?"

When five faces turned towards her with hopeful expressions, Katherine smiled. "Of course."

It was almost dark as they hurried back, and it touched her to see the Fordhams, the older of the two couples, hold hands as they sat side by side to watch the last dregs of the glorious sunset. Katherine envied them. She could almost feel Lee's embrace, almost feel his warmth steal over her. She shook her head to remove the vision and concentrated on the job at hand.

Alice came beside her.

"I will remember this day for a long time, Katherine. Thank goodness, I had a chance to do this before the condos all sold. You did the right thing when you bought this boat. I'm glad I didn't try to talk you out of it."

"You don't realize how much you've encouraged me. You're the only one I told before I bought it."

"You'll make a success of this, I'm sure. I only wish the day had lasted longer. I've never had such fun showing property." She gave Katherine's hand an affectionate squeeze.

Night arrived almost simultaneously with arrival back at the slip. While Alice and her clients disembarked, Katherine thought she saw Lee's Jeep pull out of the marina parking area. If that *was* Lee, then he wasn't at the class, either.

She decided to call the store in Fort Myers. She had seen them take calls during the class, and it was almost time for it to start.

After she said her good-byes and cleaned the boat, she dialed the number. On the second ring, a male voice that reminded her of last week's instructor answered the call.

"Is Lee Thorpe there?" she dared, with a lump in her throat.

"No, not tonight. He had business in Naples."

"Thank you. I'll call him later."

She had just hung up when her phone rang.

"Hi, Katherine—Alice again. Bet you thought you'd gotten rid of me. Look, I have to drive back to Marco. The Yorks want another look. Are you busy right now? I hate to go out alone at night with just my clients, and my husband has to work tonight or he'd go with me."

"I'd love to go. I've never been to Marco except by boat."

"Well, I'm here at the office, and I need about twenty minutes more to finish my paperwork before I pick them up at their motel. The Fordhams just left.

They signed a contract about fifteen minutes ago."

"Great work, Alice. I'll meet you at the office in about five minutes and keep you company while you finish your work. It'll be fun to get in on your doubleheader."

Katherine left her car at the office and rode with Alice to pick up the Yorks—an embarrassed couple, to say the least.

"I bet you hate people like us who can't make up their minds," Mr. York apologized.

"Not at all," Alice assured them. "Buying a home is one of the biggest decisions we make in our lives. I looked at my house four times before I finally bought it. And now I'm tempted to sell it and buy one of these condos so Katherine will take me on another boat trip."

They all laughed and had a merry time on the ride there.

Alice took them straight up to the condo under consideration, and the first thing they noted was the night view from its windows and balcony. The Yorks needed only ten minutes to make up their minds.

"Do you two need to get right back, or could we go to that restaurant we stopped at earlier and buy you girls dinner? We feel like celebrating now that we've finally made a decision," Mr. York ventured.

They all went to eat at the surprisingly crowded Captain's Cabin—clearly a popular nightspot even on a weekday night. Although the restaurant served excellent entrées, the atmosphere and quaint, nautical decor seemed the main attraction. To dine there felt like dining on board a ship. No wonder Buzzy included pictures of it in the brochure. They managed to secure a table, and the Yorks signed the contract before the waiter even arrived to take their order.

After Alice had dropped the happy couple off at their motel, she drove Katherine back to the office where she had left her car. Only by accident did Katherine see the green Jeep parked in a large, new-car lot across from the office. At night, it could easily be mistaken for one of the cars on display, but it looked like Lee's Jeep.

"Alice, would you drop me at that coffee shop up ahead?" She pointed to a cafe on the right about a block from the office. "I need to see someone there, and I can walk back to the office for my car when I'm through."

"I don't mind waiting. After all, you gave up your entire evening for me."

"No, really, I might decide to stay and chat for a while."

She hurried into the cafe and waited until Alice drove away before she started a cautious walk back towards the car lot. She felt silly and paranoid. Why would he park his Jeep there?

When she came up behind the dealership, there sat Lee's Jeep with him at the wheel. He held what looked like a fast-food coffee, and he faced the darkened real estate office with its one, lone, parked car—*hers*. Did he think she was in the office, or did he want to see who would bring her back to it? She couldn't think of any other reason for his presence there.

Hidden from his view, she made herself as comfortable as possible and grimly prepared to wait him out. A long hour passed, and he still sat there, though it looked like he had dozed off. She grew impatient and irritated. Finally, she grew bold enough to check whether he waited there because of her car.

Katherine straightened her cramped, weary legs

and circled the entire block to enter her car from the opposite side. Silently she climbed in and could see that his head still tilted sideways. Only after she started her motor did he come to attention. She drove to the marina, parked the car, and ran to a spot near the road where she could see if he followed. She had barely stepped behind cover when the Jeep came past.

He didn't drive into the lot, but slowed noticeably, probably to confirm that her car was there, and then drove away.

Somehow, the incident infuriated her. He wouldn't call her or come to see her, yet he skulked around like a criminal and watched her.

Probably because he is a criminal.

Anger and suspicion still played games with her mind as she worked on the boat the next afternoon, so she was in no mood to entertain guests when Johnny drove up. She acted hospitable and greeted him casually. He stumbled around in his conversation for a few minutes, and Katherine knew that something bothered him. Finally, without invitation, he stepped aboard the boat and reclined in one of her fishing chairs. The way he stretched out his legs told her he had settled in for a long stay.

What could she do? She could tell him to leave, but not without destroying part of the safety net that she had created. Could she use his unwelcome visit as an opportunity to convince him, beyond doubt, that she knew nothing of his dealings?

"You know, I keep wondering what made you leave Chicago and move down here. A first class looker like you must have had a load of friends up there, a lot of guy friends, I'll bet."

"Thank you for the compliment." She laughed

with feigned lightness. "I'd planned the move for a long time. All my friends knew about it."

"Yea, but Dad said you came real sudden-like." His eyes narrowed and never looked away from her face.

He's worried about that night in Chicago because he drove that speeding car that tried to kill me. His eyes give him away.

"Guess I'm an impulsive person." She laughed again to cover her nervousness. He still looked unconvinced, so she elaborated more. "My boss told me that your dad was hiring, and urged me to jump on the opportunity, since I was constantly going on about moving to Florida. I'd just had a bad week, so I was ready to listen. The cold weather and the drive to work on icy roads in all that traffic had gotten me down. You wouldn't believe the work traffic up there. A couple of nights before I left Chicago, one of our typical Chicago motorists almost ran over me—someone driving too fast for the icy conditions. I guess that sort of helped me decide that I'd had enough of long, bitter winters."

"I guess that would do it for me. I'd sure hate to live in a place like that." He looked down, his eyes hidden.

If it hadn't been so frightening, she could have laughed at how easily he followed her lead. She decided to cap off her duplicity, and then change the subject. Goose bumps traveled up her spine in spite of the hot day.

"I can't imagine a Floridian moving to Chicago. I'll never move back now that I see what it's like here. Wish I'd moved long ago, especially now that I have a boat."

Ever since the morning she eavesdropped from

her plastic prison, she guessed that Johnny was the one who had tried to run her down. Now she was certain. She doubted that Buzzy or anyone else knew about it, but she figured Johnny now followed her around mainly because of that incident, not because he worried that she would cause trouble for the bank. He feared she had recognized him. She hoped her little acting job convinced him of her ignorance.

"Yeah, I see what you mean. Speaking of boats, why'd you buy this clumsy old fishing boat?"

She laughed. "I wanted a big boat, and it's old and clumsy because I couldn't afford new and sleek."

She glanced toward the parking lot just as Lee's Jeep pulled up beside her car. He didn't get out, but paused there for a second. There was no mistaking the look of disdain on his face. He backed out before she could think to wave.

Johnny turned to see what had taken her attention away, but the Jeep had gone. He settled back again in the chair and resumed the conversation. "I understand that—"

"Johnny, I'm sorry but I have to say goodbye now," she interrupted and stood up. "I must get ready for church. A friend is waiting on me, and I'm already late. I'll see you at work."

She smiled as she stepped into her cabin and noiselessly locked the door, though she felt upset enough to cry. When Johnny's car left, she buried her head in her lap and did cry. Everything was wrong.

If Lee was mixed up in all of this, then she had put herself in worse danger. Eventually, if not already, he and Buzzy would compare notes about that Saturday morning she'd cleaned the office and hid in the trash can. Worst of all—*she had almost fallen in love with him!*

12

Dawn broke as gray and dreary as her mood, which worsened when she learned that her party of the day included Johnny again. He intended to show his client a number of properties on Marco, ones that would require a drive around the island after they arrived there by boat. When she returned from the trip, she would be off work until Monday, the only redeeming factor of the day ahead.

The water grew choppy on the trip over, rough enough to make one of the passengers slightly seasick. With hopes that the inclement weather conditions would excuse her from Johnny's motor tour, she called him aside.

"I should stay with the boat, Johnny, and keep an eye on it in case it gets stormier. I've never seen these properties you'll be showing, so my presence won't help much."

"I want pictures. Your boat will weather this fine. I checked before we left and the bad weather won't come in until this evening."

Having no choice, she followed along. When they finally finished, the weather had worsened considerably, and Johnny agreed that he should take his people back to Naples by car while she took the boat back alone.

Katherine headed towards the dock and saw that the water had grown considerably rougher, though the slate colored sky and the brisk wind blowing the palms made a magnificent picture. She wished she could wait until the weather cleared somewhat, but by then, it would be dark and conditions might grow worse. She wasn't ready for either of those possibilities.

Just as she reached the *Miss Iris*, the rain poured down in torrents. Katherine rushed to loosen the lines and noticed someone had tied them to different posts—actually one post further down. Nothing else seemed irregular, and she paid it no more mind until she headed out and noticed that the gas gauge read lower than it should. She had checked it regularly since the last discrepancy and had ascertained its accuracy, but she had no time to think about it right then. The weather had asserted its power and required her full attention.

The wind had picked up and the rain sheeted across the water. She would have to take the Intracoastal back to Naples since the Gulf would be too rough for safety. She saw no boats on the water anywhere, except a distant motorboat apparently at anchor. The sky darkened even more and the rain grew heavier. She couldn't understand that small open boat out there in the midst of the storm, but she felt better because of it. If that little boat could weather the storm, certainly the *Miss Iris* could. She increased her speed and headed towards home. When she saw that her boat could handle the conditions with no trouble, she ran the *Miss Iris* almost wide open.

Behind her, the motorboat decided to come in too, but it was still a good distance away.

About halfway home, the rain slackened somewhat, but the wind continued to be brisk. She looked astern again and could see the motorboat much clearer now. Something was familiar about it. She focused on it through the mini-binoculars she kept at the helm.

"Lee! Following me again."

Taking a closer look, she confirmed that it was the same boat that had sped past in the gulf the other day—Lee's.

"What do you think you'll learn, Mr. Thorpe?" she hollered into the wind, aware he could never hear her from that distance.

When she slowed the *Miss Iris*, he promptly slackened his speed to match. She studied him through the glasses again and increased the magnification so she could see his face clearly. His dark hair blew straight out from his head and reminded her of something, someone. An unpleasant feeling swept over her.

Katherine turned her attention back to the course and tried to place the haunting memory. Long ago, she had put away the thought that she had once seen him. She had studied his face so many times in the last few weeks that she no longer could imagine any former meeting. Now she knew why she hadn't been able to place him. She had tried to visualize him somewhere in Naples, when it had been Chicago.

She had first seen him on that terrible day at the bank. Through the binoculars, she no longer saw the Lee Thorpe she thought she knew. She saw the man in the gray suit and the blowing hair who had asked about Mr. Pinkston—the man with the real suntan and the polite *ma'am* and the mocking eyes. Why had Lee been there?

He maintained the same distance all the way. When she approached the marina, he sped past and quickly disappeared.

She *wanted* him to show up. She wanted to have it out with him, that infuriating sneak.

A couple of hours in her cabin, mulling over the situation, left her too unsettled to sleep. The rain had ceased and the wind had died down. She wanted to see how the Gulf responded to a storm. She slid into some warmer slacks and tennis shoes, and started out for the pier.

When she pulled out of the marina lot, she saw the green Jeep hidden in the shadows to the side. She wondered how many times he had waited in that same spot and she had never seen him. With freshened anger, she took a zigzag course to the pier, sometimes turning off her lights for an entire block.

Try and follow me now. How dumb do you think I am? Your Jeep sticks out like a sore thumb—and Johnny's car, too. Do you think you're clever? She wanted to shout in Lee's face. She wanted to yell at Johnny and his repulsive father, too. Her patience had vanished.

The pier did its work. An hour of ocean gazing restored her calmness. Although still scared and confused, she could go back to the boat and sleep. She turned off the headlights as she neared the marina and crept slowly towards the place where she last saw Lee. Her heart jumped at sight of the Jeep. She hadn't expected to find it still parked there.

What nerve. Must I be hounded the rest of my life by these criminals?

Lee had failed her—failed to live up to her hopes and expectations. Fury and disappointment filled her. She bore down on the gas pedal and shot through the distance that separated them. Her loud horn blast and sudden headlights preceded her stomp on the brake pedal. Her car screeched to a stop inches from his Jeep.

He jumped in his seat.

She waited for him to drive away and hoped he had learned that two could play this childish game of espionage.

Lee suddenly stepped from his Jeep, a look on his face such as she had never seen.

She became suddenly, gutlessly afraid. She slammed into reverse at the same instant that he leaned through her window and reached for her keys. She beat him away while she protectively gripped the keys and mashed the gas pedal at the same time.

He ruthlessly grabbed her hand and wrenched it away from the ignition, even as her car dragged him along. When the motor died, he still crushed her hand that held the keys.

"I'm a real fool, a real amateur next to you." His voice sounded like a hiss. "I should have believed my first hunch. You know all about this outfit, don't you? You're the innocent babe playing your smooth innocent little game." He looked down at her and laughed harshly. "I shouldn't give you this much, but for what it's worth..." he leaned close to her ear and gave her a meaningful look, "take my advice and disappear because I won't stop for sentiment." He still crushed her hand and the keys cut into her flesh. Finally he released her and walked wearily back to his Jeep without a backward look. Within seconds, he was gone.

She turned out the still glaring headlights and sat there in the dark, rubbing feeling into numb fingers. She sat there for a long time, waiting for the shaking to pass.

The masquerade had ended. He had said it right

out—*You know all about this*. She remembered that she had answered nothing, but what could she have answered—that she didn't know anything? Sure, she didn't know anything, except that they were all crooked, and they killed those who got in their way.

How had she foolishly trusted him, had actually fallen for him? She must have been insane. He had only been attentive to gain information, to fulfill the requirements of his loathsome job.

Where was the cleverness she thought she possessed—that he insinuated she possessed? She had actually believed he had genuine feelings for her. Maybe he had cared a little. He had warned her to run. Why had he? Did he mean he would kill her, or would he let Johnny do it? His last words still rang in her ears—*I won't stop for sentiment.*

In sudden panic, she wondered if he had gone to tell Buzzy. Was that what he had meant? She needed to know. With headlights off, she drove towards Buzzy's big house that she had seen only once before. She parked behind a church, four blocks away, and walked until she came in sight of his drive. No Jeep was parked there, only Buzzy's and Johnny's cars.

She stealthily crossed to the tall hedge that surrounded his yard and squeezed into its foliage to wait for Lee's arrival. They wouldn't risk a phone conversation about such a matter.

During the tense wait, she couldn't stop her mind's workings. What should she do? She had put off that question far too long. It wouldn't help to go back to Chicago because that seemed to be their headquarters. New York sounded good—to be near her mother—but she couldn't put her mother in danger. *I'll never be safe again, no matter where I go.* She deliberated there in the dark, lonely silence.

If she only knew some solid information, she could get police help. Just a name, or place or some useful piece of information—that was all she needed to put it in the hands of the authorities. She must investigate on her own. Since she was already deep in danger, what was the risk? She shouldn't have been so complacent, playing with the boat and playing at love, when she knew that crimes had happened and would continue to happen. She should have worked diligently to purge this vileness before there were more victims—before she became a victim.

She bowed her head to ask for help from the only Friend she trusted right then. *Forgive my smugness, Lord. I know I should have been seriously working, all along, to solve this mystery. If someone else has died while I hesitated, I know I share the blame. If You'll help me now, I'll do what I can to uncover this evil.*

She crept slowly around the house, half-hidden in the dripping shrubbery, and breathed a prayer of thanks that they owned no dogs. The screened in patio on the back of the house was unlit. She started to approach it for a clearer view into the house when drifting cigar smoke made her aware of a dark figure reclining on a lounge chair.

Buzzy! The smoke drifted harshly on the freshly washed night air.

Her mind went back to the ashes she had found on the *Miss Iris*—sweet smelling, not pungent like Buzzy's cigar smelled. She wondered how those ashes tied in with all the other happenings.

Katherine scooted further back under the foliage and settled down on the wet sand under the hedge. Minutes passed slowly.

The glow from his cigar faded and grew brighter by turn as he savored it. Nothing had happened by the time he finally rose from his chair some forty-five minutes later. He ambled into his house and locked the glass doors.

She struggled to rise from her uncomfortable position and rubbed feeling back into her stiff legs. Cautiously, she slipped up to the enclosure and could see the main room beyond. Though it looked dark and unoccupied, a light glowed from the right side of the house, maybe from a bedroom.

Close against the damp stucco, she followed around the house to a dimly lit window. On tiptoe she could just see through the crack where the two curtains met. Johnny sat on a couch and watched a television show. He wasn't dressed for going out, nor did he look as if he had just received any revealing message. When she traveled further along the wall to the only other lighted window, she made out Buzzy's bulky frame as he prepared for bed. That settled that.

The night's chill and dampness had penetrated her depths. She ran the entire distance back to her car. Breathless and not much warmer, she started the motor and turned on the heater to dry some of the moisture from her clothes. The car's clock said it was after eleven. That left plenty of time for a search of Buzzy's real estate office. Maybe she could find evidence there—of what nature she didn't know, but she had to try something.

With no close-by places to hide a car, she parked at a distance and started on the long walk. On her way, she checked the other places where she had seen Lee's Jeep hidden. When she had ascertained her privacy, she entered through the back door of the office.

Alone in the silent room, she watched the reflection of outside neons as they traveled across the rows of associates' desks. As the red and blue lights flashed off and on, the room rippled with moving shadows. Their brightness would never facilitate the study of papers, and she had brought no flashlight. Investigations that night would have to take place in the three rooms that sported doors. Buzzy's office seemed the obvious place to start.

With closed door and light on, she methodically sorted through each of his desk drawers but found nothing incriminating. A gun lay in the bottom right hand drawer—a vicious reminder of her risk, but unhelpful as evidence. Many business people kept guns for protection. Buzzy would own a permit for it, of course. She closed the drawer and started work on his address book.

Most of the numbers meant nothing to her, but she copied all the Chicago listings. She found her old Chicago real estate office number and Lloyd's home phone number, but she already knew that he and Buzzy were well acquainted—maybe too well acquainted, she considered. The rest of the Chicago listings looked unfamiliar.

She wearily examined a smaller desk and a couple of file cabinets on the other side of his room. The tedious work gobbled up time. When she finally came to the papers lying on his main desk, her ebbing energy told her they would have to wait.

Her body cried out for rest, for the soft bed on the boat and a few hours to forget everything, but the time for such options had run out. This problem wouldn't go away with a good night's sleep. At this point, she faced only two possible outcomes—she could expose them, or they could kill her.

The thought sobered her, and she pushed herself to make one last search—the file room. She remembered that Buzzy had sent Johnny to the cabin with something they needed to hide. That something would serve as evidence if the right hands got possession of it. Katherine needed to find that cabin. It could be one of the properties he owned, some piece of acreage with a shack on it, or something of that nature.

She leafed through an unlocked file cabinet, but realized it would take too long to search all the files. If Buzzy had filed information on such a property, she would more likely find it in one of the locked cabinets. Remembering a string of keys in Buzzy's office, she dashed back for those. When none of them fit it, she realized continued investigations would have to wait. Dawn approached, and she must leave right away and find a safe place to rest. With no hint of when Lee might act, or what he might do, she had no choice but to come back again that night as early as possible.

With her boat no longer a safe refuge, she needed to find a place to hide and rest. Iris would surely take her in, but she didn't want to involve the woman in something this dangerous. No place in Naples seemed safe. At four-thirty in the morning, she pulled into the parking lot of a shopping center in Fort Myers and opted for the front seat of her car again, too sleepy to care.

13

Fifteen minutes later, giant, predatory, beasts-on-wheels made deafening passes around the parking lot, charged scraps of paper, and swallowed aluminum cans and bottles as they sped back and forth. It seemed an eternity waiting for them to move on to another area. When the noise finally became more distant, and she started to doze off, the sound of a metal dustpan scraping against the pavement somewhere close by disturbed her rest again. Someone swept around the few cars parked there—on the search for any prey the pavement cleaning machines had missed. Not wanting anyone to see her sleeping in her car, she sat upright and waited for them to finish.

Katherine had just settled back on her inadequate bed when two cars pulled up on her right. Their drivers immediately started a noisy, raucous conversation. They laughed and carried on louder than anyone had a right to converse at that time of the morning. This time, she didn't bother to rise. The sky grew light. She had to sleep if she meant to investigate again that night. While she gazed up at her car's headliner, she mentally demanded they shut up and leave her in peace.

Sometime later, she awoke wet with sweat and painfully stiff from her inadequate bed. Her head swam, and she opened her windows to replace the heat with fresh air. Though only mid-morning, the sun had brutally assaulted her closed car.

At a small restaurant, Katherine washed her face and drank coffee until she started to feel human again. Finally, she headed back to Naples with the realization she must monitor Lee closely, now. It wouldn't do to keep him from finding her. She needed to know where he was at all times. Using her phone, she found his address and wondered why she had never tried to locate it before. Immediately she answered her own question. She had expected him to look for her—foolish romantic that she was.

When Katherine reached his neighborhood, she prepared to surpass him at his spy game. One street over from his home, she made a slow pass and peered at his house from between two residences. It looked exactly like what she would have expected—a large rustic house backed up to a canal. The yard sported more trees than grass.

With the two-car garage closed and the drive empty, she considered breaking in and searching for evidence. She might not find another opportunity. After a second pass down the street, she decided not to take the risk.

Lee could have parked his Jeep in the garage, and he seemed much more wary and capable than Buzzy or Johnny.

She would control her impatience and make do with what she could find in the office that night. Katherine's next agenda was to board the boat for a few minutes unobserved. She would have to park elsewhere and walk again. She drove past the marina and checked for the Jeep or Johnny's car. Finding neither, she drove on and parked behind her own church.

With purse and phone, she returned to the boat and ensconced herself in the cabin. The bed looked inviting, but she couldn't risk staying that long. Someone had boarded her boat while it was moored at Marco, and that could happen again. Those discrepancies might not relate to the Buzzy matter, but she must consider such a possibility until she found out differently.

She studied her list of Chicago numbers and her copy of the bank picture while she tried to reach Laura on her phone.

"Katherine, I'm glad you called. It's a wonder you got me at all. I'm making my last trip and left my phone in my purse. I heard it just as I got in my car. Sorry I haven't called, but we've been super busy. We just moved back to our house. You should see it."

"I'm so glad, Laura. You'll have to send me some pictures. So you're totally moved?"

"Yes, finally home. How are you doing? Did you move onto your boat, yet?"

"Yes, and I have loads of news, but it'll have to wait. I called to see if you had learned anything more about Jack Evans and to warn you to be very careful regarding that. The situation involves more than I realized, and I don't want to put you at risk. If you've done any checking, please don't let anyone—not anyone—know about it."

"Sounds exciting. I'm afraid I haven't learned anything. I got so busy with moving that it slipped my mind, but I have a couple of friends who work at the bank and I'll see what I can learn. I'll be super discreet, I promise. Any information in particular that you need to know?"

"Yes, I need to know when Jack Evans went to

work at the bank," Katherine said with lowered voice. "That and anything else you can find out about him, but remember that it could put you in danger—serious danger—if certain people knew you were searching for information on him. You'd have to get the information offhand—very offhand."

"Don't worry Kay. You know me. I can get information subtly when I try. I'll take no chances. It'll be fun to play private detective."

Katherine felt better after her phone call. She didn't feel so alone, and Laura had acted more like her old self—the friend she had known before the bank problem.

At least, Laura's house is fixed, and they can't take it back now.

A quick look out the door told her she was still alone. She took advantage of the opportunity and turned on the bilge pump. While that ran, she rechecked the gas gauge and found it unchanged from when she came in last time. That should serve as final proof that it worked correctly, and the logbook supported the conclusion. She need to find out why it registered too high on one occasion and too low another, and she needed explanations for some of the other irregularities she had discovered. There might be viable reasons for some of them, but not all.

Although those oddities proved that someone had boarded the boat, maybe even ran it, she needed to know who and how. She never gave her keys to anyone, except on that first trip when she gave them to Billy. The only consistency to the strange happenings was Johnny's presence on the boat during the Marco condo trips.

She packed a briefcase with a few necessities,

including a flashlight, cell phone, and her purse. That left her with just one item to carry into the office that night. She changed to fresh clothes, locked the cabin, and left.

On the other side of Naples, she found an inconspicuous parking place to relax for a while and review the situation. With her head leaned back against the headrest, she went over everything she had learned so far. She knew that Johnny Amano had committed a crime, probably murder, and probably in Naples. Afterward, he had gone to Chicago to work in a bank as Jack Evans, and there he had gotten involved in a scam, probably with Laura's insurance money, his own trivial deal for personal gain.

And he tried to run over me because I had caused him trouble, and might cause more trouble if I stayed alive.

Besides those facts, she had developed many viable, but vague conjectures. Some big boss in Chicago, someone over Buzzy and Johnny, gave the orders. Lloyd might be involved. Lee seemed caught up in it. Businesses might be involved—the bank in Chicago, Lloyd's and Buzzy's real estate offices, and maybe the eleven Marine World stores.

If she could fit everything together, she could take it to the police. Who would have dreamed that Laura's bank trouble could land her in something so heinous?

Katherine rested and waited for darkness. She tried to plan future actions, but soon realized the futility of working out any strategy. She had only the night hours ahead to find something that would show her what to do next. If she found nothing, she would try again the next night.

Impatient to start, she drove past both houses. Buzzy was at home, but Johnny's car and Lee's car were both gone. Risk or no risk, she must start—every minute counted. She parked in the same place as the night before and made a cautious, roundabout trek to the office. After a brief pause in the bushes beside the dumpster, she hastily entered through the back.

With only a flashlight for illumination, she started in the main room and kept watch through the windows as she worked. If a car showed up, she could exit before anyone came in. She would save the rooms with doors until after midnight when there was less chance of an unwelcome caller.

She found nothing noteworthy in any of the associates' desks and figured that only Buzzy and Johnny were involved. At midnight, she closed herself in the file room and studied all the accessible papers. Six files contained papers on recent purchases by Buzzy. She quickly copied them. With a paper clip and a small pocketknife, she worked on the locked files. After fifteen minutes of fruitless labor, she gave it up as a waste of time.

In Buzzy's office, she copied most of the messages on his desk. One message from Lloyd had a recent date. Most of the others seemed unimportant, but she copied them for future reference. She noted the bank clipping had disappeared. In his wastebasket, she found more messages and put those in her briefcase.

His desk clock told her it was going on three o'clock. She hadn't checked maps and plats yet, hadn't gotten into the locked files, and hadn't even checked behind the refrigerator for a safe of some sort. The regular office safe was in Buzzy's office, and she had searched, unsuccessfully, for its combination. With a sinking feeling, she realized she would have to come back and work another full night. She hadn't collected any information she could take to the police.

Discouraged, she moved into the kitchen and examined the refrigerator with the aid of her flashlight. It fit snugly between cabinets, but she could probably pull it out if she had enough time and wanted to take the risk. Not only was the kitchen visible through the back door, but someone might come in when she had it out in the middle of the room. She should have attempted that job earlier, though she had no safecracking abilities if she did find a safe behind it.

She stashed everything in her briefcase and turned off the flashlight. It seemed she got nowhere except wearier, and full of unanswered questions. If she didn't find anything tomorrow, what could she do? Had Lee told Buzzy? Would Lee do something to her? And what about work on Monday? She couldn't dare show up, and she couldn't dare not show up.

From the back door of the office the streets looked deserted—no cars or people in sight. She rested her tired forehead against the doorframe for a minute before silently sliding out. She had just locked it and set the alarm when an arm clamped round her shoulders and a hand came over her mouth.

14

Katherine gave a muffled scream in spite of the hand. She fought wildly, broke free, and leapt away from her adversary, only to have him catch her by the foot and send her to a hard landing on the ground beside the waste receptacle.

She kicked her way free again and ran a few yards before her pursuer tripped her and sent her sprawling. When she landed face down in the dirty sand, her arm struck a broken piece of board that had escaped the dumpster.

Desperately she grabbed the wood and rolled to her back. Even in the darkness, she could make out her assailant's outline. She swung the board across his face, and when he groaned, she brought it down again—on his head. From her awkward position on the ground, she couldn't put the force into it that she needed. She heard his second groan of pain, but she hadn't stopped him, and before she could squirm away, he was on top of her. She screamed and fought him.

He tore the piece of wood from her hands and threw it aside, where it made a metallic thump as it connected with the side of the dumpster.

She twisted sideways and grabbed the briefcase. With both hands wielding it, she brought it down on his head and swiftly followed that with a handful of sand in his face. She had almost managed to roll free when he caught her wrist and pinned it to the ground above her head. With her free hand, she tried to swing the briefcase at him again. He caught that wrist, too, and pinned it with the other one above her head, while he placed his free hand over her mouth so she couldn't scream again. He outweighed her, and her struggles failed to dislodge him.

They both breathed audibly, and she could hear the thump of his heart.

"Hush...hush...I won't hurt you." It was Lee's voice, not Johnny's. When he took his hand from her mouth, she screamed again.

"Shh. I'm not going to hurt you, I won't hurt you," he repeated and pressed his hand against her cheek.

She couldn't stop the tears. "You *have* hurt me." She struggled to break free.

"I'm sorry, but I need whatever you have in that briefcase." He released her hands, but continued to pin her down.

"Never," she gasped furiously, and grabbed the briefcase handle. She swung it again, but did little damage. "I've worked all night. My life depends on it. You'd have to kill me to get it."

"I'm not in the habit of killing people. I'm not like—"

"You're friends are! Are you any different?" she challenged hotly.

"Friends? What friends?"

"Your friends...your colleagues—partners-in-crime—whatever you call them."

"Who? Tell me who?"

"Johnny. And Buzzy," she gasped. "You fraud. Just try and fool me again." She struggled to push him away but couldn't move him.

"Answer one question," he demanded sternly.

139

"What were you doing in this office with Johnny and Buzzy that morning, that morning when I caught you in the act? Don't pretend you don't know what I'm talking about."

This is it, she thought, but her fear had evaporated. She felt only righteous indignation—and regret, so much regret.

"Of course I remember the morning. I was hiding in the garbage barrel in the kitchen," she said proudly.

Silence met her bold proclamation, and then Lee's laughter rocked both of them. Was he demented? If he pulled out a gun to shoot her, it wouldn't have surprised her. But this?

"I heard everything they said, and I intend to use it," she added with vehemence. "You'll find I'm not so easy to kill, after all. Maybe you should be the one to disappear."

While he still laughed, she brought the briefcase down on his head again, but it didn't stop his laughter, and she still couldn't move him off of her.

He gently pushed her hair away from her wet eyes and sandy forehead.

"We'll use it—Kate. *We* will. I've just discovered we're on the same team."

She peered up at his face and tried to read his dark glistening eyes, but could find no meaning to his words. Her arms were too dead to raise the briefcase again, but she tried to struggle free.

"Kate." he shook her gently, "Listen, Kate. I'm investigating Johnny and Buzzy. I mean to put them in jail. I thought you worked for them."

"I do work for them." She looked up at him confused. "I work at their real estate office."

"I don't mean that kind of work. I thought you

might be involved with them criminally. And now I realize that you thought I was one of their cohorts, didn't you?"

"Aren't you?"

"I'm not! Please try to believe me. Let's go some place private, and I'll explain everything." He lifted his weight off her and knelt in the sand. "We're going to sink their rotten little boat, Kate, you and I, together."

Comprehension came slowly. "Boat? It's not a boat. It's an ocean liner...an entire fleet."

"We'll sink them all."

"I won't have the strength to sink anything if you keep fighting with me." She brushed a sandy hand across her eyes.

"I'm sorry. I'm so sorry, Kate...but it's almost as much fun as taking you out to eat."

"You broke my briefcase." She showed him the barely attached handle.

"You think that's bad, you should see my head. I think I got the worst of it." He rose and held out his hand.

She laughed softly as he helped her to her feet. When he saw what a struggle it was for her to move, he scooped her and the briefcase into his arms and carried both to his Jeep.

"Where's your car?" he asked as he set her down to open the Jeep door.

"Behind the nursery."

"I'd better have someone bring it. You're not—"

"I can drive," she said with energy she didn't feel.

He drove straight to her car and helped her from the Jeep.

"Promise you'll follow me."

He stood by her open car door and waited. When

no response came, he got the briefcase from his Jeep, put it on the seat beside her, and looked at her questioningly.

"I'll follow, but don't drive fast." She couldn't subdue a snicker. "It'll be nice to follow that Jeep for a change instead of it following me."

He grinned sheepishly. "Sorry, Ma'am."

At his house they both drove into the garage, and he closed the door behind them.

He used a small flashlight to find his house key and opened the side door. "Come in. I'll have the light on in a minute, as soon as I draw the curtains."

When he did switch on a lamp, Katherine still stood in the doorway, legs tremulous and briefcase cradled against her chest. She knew how haggard she must look, but couldn't summon enough strength to move.

He carried her to his bed where he managed to pull back the coverings with his fingers as he gently lowered her onto the cool sheets. He removed the briefcase from her grasp and laid it on the bed beside her.

"My shoes."

She tried to sit upright and remove them, but her limbs reacted sluggishly.

He shoved her back onto the pillow, removed the shoes, and pulled the covers up to her neck. He walked into the adjoining room and dropped down on the sofa.

They both came startlingly awake a few minutes before nine o'clock that morning, when the briefcase rang.

Lee rushed into the room, and they both fumbled hopelessly to get Katherine's cell phone before the caller hung up.

Katherine finally reached it. "Hello."

"Katherine, I was wonderin' could ya come to dinner today, or do ya have to work after all?" Iris asked.

"I'm not at the boat, Iris. It doesn't look like I'll have the day off, but thank you for thinking of me. I'll see you in the morning." Katherine put the phone aside, and they both laughed over their confused rush.

"Was that the woman I saw you with at church?"

"Yes, Captain Dale's wife—a dear friend of mine. Captain Dale is the one who taught me almost everything I know about boats." With mischief in her voice she added, "Of course I did learn a little in your class."

"Yes, I remember the doodles," he said reproachfully.

She chuckled and within seconds, she fell back asleep. When she awoke again, it was noon, and someone tormented her face with a cold, wet washcloth. Coming out of the depths of sleep, she suddenly recognized the hazel eyes that laughed down at her.

"Ugh," she uttered, and pushed the rag away as she struggled to sit up in bed. "I'm stiff. Umm! Do I smell coffee...and food? I'm starved!"

"No one comes to my table with a dirty face like yours. And your hair's full of sand, and your arms and hands and—"

"I wonder why." she interrupted with meaningful look. Remorse filled her when she saw the wicked looking wound that traveled across the bridge of his nose and down his cheek. "Y-your...your face."

"Your work." He rubbed his hand across it and

grimaced. "I guess I shouldn't feed you after all."

She looked down at her right hand where he had crushed the keys into it. What luck—a tiny, bluish-purple bruise remained. She held it out for his sympathy and added mock tears.

"All right, all right, I give in. You can eat."

"I need a shower first, if you don't mind." She almost lost her balance when she tried to stand.

He caught her arm to steady her. "You'd better stay dirty until you get some food in you. By the way, how much sleep have you had lately?"

"Night before last I had a couple of hours on the front seat of my car."

"I thought it might be like that. We have plenty of talking to do, but it will keep. Let's eat, and I warn you—all I can cook is sea food. These are supposed to be scrambled eggs, and that's supposed to be toast," he said and helped her to a seat at the table.

She tasted a forkful of egg while he watched her with a worried expression.

"They taste wonderful. Eggs on the half shell." She smiled and removed a piece of shell. "And the dark brown and yellow color you've accomplished—most unusual. You'll have to tell me how you do that."

He looked at her dubiously. "It's easy. Mine always look like that. I heat the skillet on high for a few minutes and then throw the eggs into the grease. I discovered that if I use a lot of grease, the eggs don't stick, and I don't have to clean the skillet. I generally keep a cover for the skillet close by in case they catch fire. If that happens, I get a little more of the brown tone."

"I'll have to try that sometime." She smiled and took a bite of burnt toast.

After a meal and each of them taking a shower, they sat back on his sofa to enjoy their coffee.

Katherine looked at him accusingly. "Why have you been following me?"

"Because you're better looking than Buzzy and Johnny." He grabbed a sofa pillow and held it in front of him as if he expected a new attack.

"Lee!"

"OK. I had hoped you'd lead me to some answers." He tossed the pillow to her.

"What sort of answers?"

"I've been investigating your real estate office for the past few months. I thought they were mixed up in something...bad, extremely bad. I had reached a dead end until you and Johnny showed up here on almost the same day."

"And that made you suspicious of me?" She leaned forward and put down her almost empty cup.

"Not at first. I had been suspicious of Johnny for quite a while, but I couldn't find him. No one knew where he was, or else no one would tell. Then I got a hint that he might work at a certain bank in Chicago. It wasn't much of a hint, but it was all I had to go on, so I went up there to see for myself."

"And you met a rude customer who came out of Mr. Pinkston's office. I apologize, but I was extremely angry with Mr. Pinkston, and then you...you thought I was his secretary."

"So, you did remember me from that day." He brought the coffee pot over and refilled their cups.

"Not until you followed the *Miss Iris* home in the rain and wind. I looked at you through my binoculars, and your hair was horizontal—like it had been that day in Chicago. Did you discover anything while you were up there?"

"I discovered I should have taken a heavier coat. That's about all. I couldn't get any information on Johnny, so I came back. And then Johnny showed up and so did this girl in a car with an Illinois tag."

"And you thought we arrived together?"

"I thought it might mean something. I followed you and learned you frequented the beach in the early mornings—and that you were the same girl I'd seen at the Chicago bank. That's when I planned to get to know you better, but I wasn't really suspicious of you until that morning you ran past me from your office. You looked so guilty."

"But you were spying on me, then."

"I was spying on the Amanos. I'd gone out early to fish and saw them pull into the office. I was curious about what they might be up to at that hour of the morning. You were the surprise—coming out right after them."

"May I ask what this bad thing is that you think they did?"

"I guess I owe you that." He put down his cup. "This has to do with my aunt. I've mentioned her to you—Aunt Molenda. She was one of the few relatives I had left, and we'd always been close. She planned to move nearer to me—didn't tell me outright that she was moving to Naples, but I could tell what she had in mind. She was always very independent and liked to run her own affairs. Well...I was on a three-month diving expedition—I have projects like that from time to time—and she had my expedition address and wrote regularly. The last thing I got from her was this."

He handed Katherine a worn card with small, attractive handwriting.

Dear Lee,

By the time you're back in home port, you'll have a new neighbor—not close enough to be a nuisance but close enough to share dinner and talk now and again.

Found a lovely little condo today that I can just afford right now with the discount I get for paying cash. Closing this afternoon!

Love, Molenda

"You haven't heard from her since this?" Her grip on the card became tense.

"Not a thing. And she was in perfect health—intelligent too, but a trifle naive about business matters. I guess she wanted to surprise me."

Immediately all business, Katherine looked at the envelope.

"It has a date. Did you check old newspapers and the Internet to see what they advertised at that time? Did you check the real estate Multiple Listing Service?"

"Affirmative to both questions."

"It's a Naples postmark. There's not much chance she would buy in another town—especially since she was closing the sale that afternoon. Did you check Marco?"

"Checked everything in this area of the state."

"Was her money gone from her bank account?"

"She had about four thousand dollars left in her account. The bank's been very helpful. They said she'd just transferred her money to their bank. Consequently, no one knew her. She personally withdrew forty four thousand dollars—in cash. When the teller suggested a cashier's check, or something safer, my aunt explained that the real estate office had arranged for a security agent to escort her to her closing. That was all the bank knew, and it was so like my aunt. She was tight-lipped about her affairs. I checked security agencies. It was obviously a phony agent."

"Did you come up with any leads regarding condos?"

"Here's the list of ones available at the time. The most obvious choice was a one-bedroom condo near Golden Gate for forty-seven thousand. It was a large ad and the real estate office was Amano's."

"That sounds about right," Katherine agreed. "Since she supposedly got a discount, it could easily come out to about the sum she withdrew from the bank. Or the salesperson she contacted could have made up any amount for a cash discount price." She suddenly shivered and tears filled her eyes as she remembered Buzzy and Johnny's conversation. She looked up at Lee.

"It's all right," he said sadly. "Months ago convinced myself she was dead. She was a saintly woman, and it was my loss, not hers. I would've loved having her close by. Once I invited her to live with me, but she wouldn't consider it—didn't want to impose. She had always lived by herself."

"It would have been Johnny," Katherine said simply.

Lee's eyes smoldered with unspoken fury.

15

"Johnny! My gut feeling told me he had something to do with it, Kate."

"He had everything to do with it." She looked down, trying to decide where to begin. "There's a lot to tell, but let me start with what I know for sure about Johnny."

"That he's Jack Evans when he's in Chicago? And that he worked at that bank there, just like I'd first figured?"

"Yes, and also that he did something despicable, for monetary gain, directly before he left for Chicago. That's why Buzzy sent him up there—to protect him in case of discovery."

"But why did he come back? Did he think the heat was off?" Lee spat the words out and tightened his fists.

"Partly, I guess, but mainly because he became involved in a new scheme in Chicago—small money, ridiculously insignificant, but it almost exposed something bigger that the bank was involved in." Katherine filled him in on all the details of the bank problem and her involvement with it. When she related the details of her narrow escape from Johnny's car and explained how Lloyd had secured her a job with Buzzy, Lee's eyes narrowed.

"They really shipped you out of there in a hurry, didn't they?"

"I rather had that feeling at the time. I think it's possible that Lloyd Lucas is involved, but that's just conjecture. What I'm going to tell you now would get me killed if any of them knew. It's not conjecture; it's what I heard with my own ears." She related all she heard from inside the garbage barrel.

Lee shook his head in amazement. "No wonder you looked startled when you saw me there." He buried his face in his hands and groaned.

"Yes, and that made you suspicious of me, so you played up to me for information," she said accusingly, thinking of their pleasant times together at the restaurant and the beach.

"Just like you did me," he answered.

"Like I did with you."

Lee rose with a deep frown on his face. He paced back and forth, apparently lost in thought. "We need to get you away from here, far away. You need police protection."

"But Lee, I didn't actually hear anything that would help much. I don't know who the boss is. I don't know what their business is. I've wanted to go to the police, but I figured they couldn't do anything with the foggy bit of information I had to offer." She looked down at the briefcase before looking back up at Lee with some degree of excitement. "Now, with what you've just added, I know a heap more, don't I?"

"Considerably." he said dryly. "Listen Kate, I've been working with an FBI agent for the last two months. We haven't gotten anywhere. Now you come here and almost have it figured."

The sudden praise made her hope she wasn't blushing.

"I can still cast better than you." He ducked the

pillow she threw and immediately became serious again. "I'd like you to go with me and meet this man. I want you to give him all the information you just gave me."

"I would love to do that."

"Good. Now what else do you have suspicions about? Anything?"

She opened the briefcase and showed him the information she collected.

"My friend, Laura, is trying to get more information about Johnny—Jack Evans to her. She's the one who had the bank problem in Chicago. Tonight, I planned to go back and look at maps and try again to get into those locked files. I also thought I'd investigate behind that refrigerator. After that, I meant to check at the courthouse and see what names I could find on deeds and such, and maybe locate the cabin Buzzy and Johnny mentioned. And I intended to go back to Buzzy's house and see if I could overhear anything."

"You what? You went to Buzzy's house?"

"Night before last...in his bushes...and at his windows."

"Do you realize what risk you took?" he asked roughly.

"Do you realize you'd just told me to disappear, or else? I didn't know if you intended to kill me or if you'd get Johnny to do it. I was trying to save my life by getting information. I came by your house, too."

He looked astonished. "What a mess. Did I cause all that? What haven't you done yet, besides the list you just gave me of pending activities?"

"I've done nothing, except try and convince Buzzy and Johnny I'm totally unsuspecting. I thought I'd succeeded until I found you following me."

"Do they have any clue of your involvement…besides when you helped your friend in Chicago?"

"None whatsoever. I'm sure no one saw me enter or leave the office the last two nights."

"Excuse me a minute. I need to call Rob. He's the agent I told you about."

He reached the man immediately and arranged to meet with him in a couple of hours.

"Lee, I need to get back to my boat, now. I've been on the run since Thursday and need to do a few things. I especially need clean clothes."

"I don't think you should go back to your boat, back to work, or anywhere else. Surely you realize you're in danger?"

"I would be in danger if they knew I'd overheard their conversation that morning, but now that I know you're not involved with them, I feel safe enough."

"I highly doubt you are, but we'll talk with Rob about it. There's one other thing that bothers me. I think you should call your friend, Laura, and tell her to cease on the information hunt."

"I agree. She was my only hope, or I'd never have involved her." Katherine tried unsuccessfully to reach Laura.

"You can try her later. Let's swing by your boat so you can do whatever needs done. Leave your car here and ride with me to Fort Myers. We'll meet Rob there."

****

Halfway to Fort Myers, Katherine's phone rang.

"Laura? Where are you now?"

"I'm at a restaurant. We're ready to eat, but I

thought I'd give you what information I've gathered so far."

"Laura, make sure no one can hear you."

"No one's near. My, this is exciting!"

"Laura, listen to me, it's so exciting that I want you to take every scrap of paper that has anything to do with this and burn them, or flush them, as soon as you can. I don't want you to check on anything else, and if anyone asks about me, don't give even a hint about this. Just try to forget everything I asked you."

"Can I tell you what I've already found out, before I start forgetting everything?" She giggled nervously.

"Yes, go ahead if you're still alone." She put her phone on speakerphone so Lee could hear the conversation.

"Well first, Jack Evans went to work in the bank around the middle of February. Some of the guys there didn't like him, but he had a gorgeous new black car that was the envy of many. He liked to spend money, too. I have a friend who's a teller there, and she actually got on the subject by herself—well, I may have led her a little. I think she had a crush on him. She kept talking about how tall and good-looking he was—great body and all that. Once I got her started, I just kept my mouth shut and listened.

"Also, when I met with Mr. Pinkston a short while ago to make changes in my house insurance, he told me a little about Jack Evans, though he didn't mention his name. He told me that the insurance goof was the employee's only error, and that he didn't want to publicize it because he knew the man's family and didn't want to cause them embarrassment. He said the bank let him quit, instead of firing him, and that he'd moved away because he was ashamed."

"Him? Ashamed? That's a hard picture to conjure up."

"That's all I've had a chance to check."

"That's enough. What you've just told me will help enormously. Now remember what I said about destroying everything. I'll talk with you later about all this. Thanks loads. Goodbye, Laura."

"Great work." Lee said with enthusiasm. "That date coincides with everything else that's happened. And her tip about the vehicle could be our best evidence to date. Rob can discreetly find out what Johnny drove. According to the conversation you overheard, it was a new purchase with my aunt's money. When Rob knows the make and model, he can have people check into sales at that time, both in this area and in Chicago. He has the manpower and connections for that type of work."

They met with Rob Preston in an unpretentious office in Fort Myers. The small, slightly balding man looked about fifty and acted polite and composed. No one would ever have pegged him as an FBI agent. When Katherine gave him all the papers she had collected, he carefully labeled them and put them in a file that already bulged with documents.

Katherine related everything that she knew and everything that had happened.

He taped her conversation and took notes at the same time. Occasionally he would stop her to ask a pertinent question. His perfect poker face never changed until Katherine described the garbage can incident. He grinned and shook his head. When she had finished he turned to Lee.

"I'm not sure how to advise you. Katherine needs protection, but if she disappears right now, it might ruin everything. They might become cautious and — "

"I don't want to stop until this is finished," Katherine broke in. "With what I know, I'd never feel safe again."

"Actually, you wouldn't be," Rob agreed. "This involves more than two or three people, more than a handful. We need to come down on the entire operation at once, if possible."

"Is it a real estate scam?" Katherine asked.

Rob looked down at his papers, and Lee walked over to a window and looked out.

"It may involve real estate," Rob said, noncommittally, after a minute's silence.

She guessed they knew more and it irritated her. After all, she had risked the most danger and had trusted them with all her information.

Rob looked questioningly at her.

"You still work for Big Buzzy and still have a key to his office, right?"

"Yes, but..."

"It wouldn't be breaking in, it wouldn't even require a search warrant, if you brought a couple of prospective buyers to your office some evening to discuss real estate, would it?"

She looked at him in amusement.

His face showed no emotion except for a slight twinkle deep in his eyes.

"I have a busy real estate schedule and rarely have any daytime hours free. I could possibly make time for you if we set up an appointment for very late in the day, say around midnight. Would that do?"

"That would do nicely. How about tomorrow night? Can you meet with two of your clients then?"

"That sounds perfect."

"I want to speed things up before it becomes too dangerous for you. I'll put some people to work right away on this new information you've given me. Now—I think you two should avoid hanging around together for a while, especially when you're in Naples. We believe they already know Lee's been snooping around."

"No doubt. That Jeep of his sticks out like a red bikini," Katherine said, not able to resist a taunt.

After she and Rob enjoyed a good laugh at Lee's expense, Rob turned to Katherine.

"Keep your phone with you at all times. I'll give you a number to memorize. Call me if you find the slightest bit of information, even if you think it's unimportant. Call if you feel you're in any danger whatsoever. Give your location first in case you don't have time for more. I want you and Lee to continue your daily schedules as naturally as possible—no sneaking around at this point. That especially goes for you, Lee." He gestured towards Lee's beat-up face. "It seems you have a tendency to run into things in the dark."

"Don't I, though."

"I think you both realize what kind of people we are investigating. You know they wouldn't hesitate to perform any act to protect themselves. Johnny, especially, has no code of morals. That fact, coupled with his unpredictability, makes him extremely dangerous. We have almost put this together, so don't either of you do anything foolish. Lee, I'll call you with instructions about our real estate meeting tomorrow night. I'll probably bring along a search warrant as a precaution. Keep an eye on Katherine, but not too closely."

On the trip back to Naples, Katherine had just dozed off when her phone rang again.

"Hey, Miss Katherine, glad I could reach you. Need you to take a party out Monday at one o'clock. It looks like we've scheduled a full week of trips. You know, my dear, this is the quickest we've ever sold a new condo development, and it's all because of your efforts."

"I'll be ready for them. Thank you, Mr. Amano. I'm glad my boat helps."

"Oh, by the way, Katherine. Things aren't so formal here as in Chicago. Just call me Buzzy."

"Thank you Bu—goodbye." She looked helplessly at Lee. "That's the second time he's asked me to call him Buzzy. I just can't."

"So he's Buzzy now? Good catch, Kate."

"Where's that board?"

"No, not again. No girl will ever look at me if you pulverize my face again."

"Oh? Do they look at you now?" she asked coolly. She was irritated with him, not just because of his pretended interest in her to gain information, but because he kept something back when she had divulged everything. Guilt was clearly written on his face—even on Rob's expressionless face. They didn't trust her to act discreetly. If anyone gave away secrets, it wouldn't be her.

Conversation dwindled after that. They talked trivialities, but it was as if a wall had sprung up between them. It had turned dark before they arrived back at Lee's place, so Katherine promptly left and returned to the boat.

She sank onto her bed, thankful to be home. An immense burden had been lifted—Lee was innocent.

She had a friend now, however mortifying it felt to realize his advances meant nothing. Still, her lips burned at thought of his last kiss.

Had just fourteen hours passed since his saving revelation had left her stunned and too emotionally drained to react—that very morning, lying there in the sand by the dumpster? It seemed eons...and eons...

16

While she and Iris sat together on the church pew the next morning, she noticed a sudden stir to their right. Katherine looked around just as Lee sat down beside her. Although he looked straight ahead, he found her hand and for a second held it in his warm grasp.

She whispered to him out of the corner of her mouth. "You've broken Rob's rule. We're not supposed to hang around together. You'll never make a good agent."

"I don't think we need to worry here. Besides, I was lonely."

Near the end of the service, he nudged her. "Can you meet me at Doctor's Pass as soon as church lets out?"

She nodded an affirmative.

"Park somewhere inconspicuous—somewhere you can leave your car for a while. And wear a swimsuit."

He left before she could reply. She understood now why she never saw him after church. He must always leave early.

When she arrived at Doctor's Pass, Lee stood at the water's edge, not far from the blue-and-silver flecked speedboat she had seen before. He was accompanied by two others—a young man and a very attractive woman. The woman seemed very interested in Lee. Everyone wore swimwear.

"Kate's going with us today as an observer," Lee explained to the others. "She may start a diving class later on. Soon as Jim arrives, we'll start out." He drew Katherine aside and spoke in an undertone. "I thought this would serve as a good way to keep an eye on you and not get in trouble with Rob."

"And who's to keep an eye on you?" She stared at the swimsuit-clad woman.

"I'm sure I'll find someone if you won't."

"I haven't eaten yet," she said, ignoring his hint

"Why didn't you eat before you came?"

"I thought you would take me to eat. You always do."

"You're spoiled."

"You said to meet you here right after church, remember?" She folded her arms.

"Why can't I ever win? We'll find you something to eat later. Did you wear a suit? We have to wade out a ways before we climb aboard. By the way, this is just a beginner's class, so don't feel intimidated."

As soon as she had slipped off her beach cover-up, she discovered Lee's gaze riveted on her new navy-blue swimsuit.

"Ready to go?" she asked, embarrassed, and folded the jacket away in her bag.

"I can't believe you clean up so...ouch, nicely," he said as she elbowed him in the ribs.

Lee boated to an area of sparkling clear water where they could view all varieties of sea life in the depths, even the shells resting on the ocean floor. Katherine listened to his instructions and found them immensely interesting. When the others started to practice diving techniques, she went off by herself and snorkeled around the area.

"Have you ever found a junonia on one of your diving trips?" she asked when Lee swam near.

"Why a junonia?"

"I want to find one for Iris. She needs one for her wonderful shell collection."

"I'll check into it for you," he said and swam off to aid a student.

The class soon ended, and he dropped the students off at the pass.

When Katherine started to climb out, Lee took hold of her arm.

"Can you run by my place with me for a few minutes? We can rob my refrigerator, and you can see a different part of the bay. I have another group to take out in a little while."

The trip back gave new meaning to the word run. From Doctor's Pass to Gordon Pass, he ran the motor wide open. Her hair wanted to leave her head. Never had she ridden in a boat of such speed—not even when she boated with her speed-crazy Chicago friends.

Lee slowed his engine for their ride down the bay, and she soon discovered that his dock wasn't far past her marina.

"Could you see what you can find to eat? I have to make some phone calls and do a few things," he said when they entered his kitchen.

"It looks like you have a pan of soup in here," she said while rummaging.

"No...don't use that. Better yet, throw it out. I experimented, and my experiment didn't come out like I expected."

"What kind of soup?" she asked and sniffed it curiously.

"I think it's some...Alaskan recipe. I call it yuk-yuk."

"OK, I'm convinced. Do whatever you have to do, and I'll see what I can scrounge up."

The refrigerator's contents represented typical bachelor fare. He obviously didn't cook often. She had set out a meager lunch when Lee returned and placed a junonia on the table in front of her.

Surprised, she picked it up. "A junonia? How lovely. And it's absolutely perfect. Would you know where I might find one?"

"This one's for Iris. It sat in my garage for years—along with countless other shells—and now it has a real home. It'll make me happy to know that it will give someone pleasure."

"Thank you. She'll love it. I'll give it to her today." Katherine thrilled with the thought.

"Now, for more serious news—I just talked with Rob. He'll come this evening and we'll all go to your office in his car. In other words, tonight is the night. Would you like to stay out of this?"

"And let you men bungle everything and ultimately get me killed?"

"OK. Come back here before nine and put your car in my garage. Watch close for snoopers. If anyone follows you, call me on your phone, and we'll figure what to do."

"Should I bring anything?"

"No. You'll show Rob around. He'll do all the work, and I'll keep watch. I guess I don't need to tell you about the risk."

"Sorry about dinner," he apologized as he sat down to eat.

"You realize there are only so many ways to fix

bologna? I could cut the sandwiches in triangles, rectangles, or squares. Or I could cut off the bread crusts and—"

"You've done well...you've done well, my dear," he interrupted

"I'll fix you a real feast after we make it through this trouble. After all, it is my turn. Let's take these sandwiches with us so you're not late for your students."

When they arrived at the pass, two students waited at the water's edge—attractive young women in bikinis.

"Really, Lee." Katherine raised her eyebrows.

"All part of the job," he said sheepishly.

"I don't want to keep you from your work. I'll see you tonight."

She took her leave of the diving party and drove straight to Iris's with the shell.

"My land, Katherine. Wherever did ya find it?" Iris's hand trembled in excitement as she took the shell.

"It's a gift from Lee Thorpe—the man who sat with us at church this morning. He's a diver, and I'm taking navigation classes from him."

Iris reverently placed it on the glass shelf and stood there taking in the effect of the new addition to her collection. At length, she turned around. "He's a nice lookin' man. I knew he was a seaman as soon as I laid eyes on him," Iris said confidently.

"How would you know that?"

"I don't rightly know. It's somethin' in the eyes. I can always tell a seaman. Oh, did I tell ya that I had May Johnson and Sarah over yesterday? They set a spell with me. They loved my shells, and I gave them a few of my extras. I spend a heap'a time just lookin' at them myself—now that they're out where I can see them." She gazed at them with a far off look on her face. "They're all full of memories."

Without asking, Katherine could tell she meant memories of happier times. A shadow hung over Iris. She had responded beautifully to Katherine's friendship, and she was genuinely happy with her new/old friends and her new/old church, but she kept her reserve. Katherine was glad she could bring a speck of happiness into Iris's bleak life. She cherished their friendship immensely. An unspoken kinship bound them together, and they understood each other.

"Will you come with me some day on one of my boat trips?" Katherine ventured.

"Just ask me and see how quick I get ready," the old woman said curtly.

Katherine laughed in surprise.

"We'll take a trip soon, then."

17

Midnight found Katherine riding in a nondescript car with Lee, Rob, and another man called James. They had gone over material and plans for almost three hours at Lee's house and were well prepared for their night's work. They left the car at the dealership across from the office and cautiously entered through the kitchen door.

Rob and James immediately pulled out the refrigerator while Lee placed himself at the front windows to keep watch. The expected safe was there in the wall and it took James less than twenty minutes to open it. He and Rob examined the contents.

Katherine kept watch at the back door. It contained a fair amount of money, but nothing obviously incriminating. They also swabbed some dust from inside and sealed it as evidence. They took pictures of the contents and recorded serial numbers before putting everything back as it was before.

"Now, where does he keep the locked file cabinets, Katherine?" Rob asked.

Katherine led them to the file room where they could work behind closed doors.

"Katherine, these will take a while. Would you use this camera and take photographs here in the main room? Start with Johnny's desk and photograph each desk's nameplate, name card, or some identifying paper on the desk before you begin to take photos of

Jean James & Mary James

address book pages or other documents. Remember to put everything back exactly as it was. If you notice anything else interesting as you go along, photograph that, too."

The agents completed their task before Katherine finished hers, so she showed them the room with the maps and plats. They worked in there and took more pictures and notes while she finished.

Finally, they all went into Buzzy's office while Lee continued to keep watch. They spent a longer time there and took pictures of everything—including the gun she had seen earlier. She would have enjoyed the night if she hadn't felt so dreadfully aware of the danger. A few minutes after four o'clock, they left.

Back at Lee's house, they drank coffee and talked.

"We'll put people to work on this information within an hour," Rob said. "We'll locate the properties Big Buzzy owns and the corporations he's involved with. Hopefully, we'll locate some structure that can be identified as a cabin, and we'll probably find that vehicle purchase before evening if Johnny purchased it in this state. Actually, by evening we should know more about everything. The agents at the Chicago end of this have worked around the clock ever since you gave us that information yesterday. I want you both to stay cool. Continue to act as normal as possible."

Katherine left Lee's house at the same time the agents left. The sun had just come up when she arrived back at the Miss Iris to get a few hours of sleep before that day's party arrived.

All too soon, the real estate agent showed up with his prospects. Aware that any trip might be her last for a while, she gave thanks the associate wasn't Johnny. She would get what enjoyment she could out of the day.

The trip itself wasn't noteworthy, but while they dined at the restaurant, she saw Billy again. She got the impression he managed the restaurant, or was at least someone high-up in authority. She couldn't help but wonder why he tended the condo dock those two days. He and Johnny also seemed very well acquainted. Late that afternoon, she called Rob and told him all she knew about Billy.

"It may not have anything to do with this investigation, but you said to call."

"Everything's important. Call on everything. I need to meet with you and Lee, probably sometime tomorrow."

"I have to take a party to Marco in my boat tomorrow. I usually go to Lee's class in Fort Myers on Tuesday evenings—when I get back early enough, that is."

"Even if you get back late, go to the class, and we'll meet afterward. I'll call Lee now. Remember, call immediately if something bothers you, or even if something just seems slightly strange."

Tuesday night she and Lee met Rob at the same office as before.

Rob had a pile of papers in front of him and motioned them to sit.

"We've about put this together. The Chicago end has done well. They have corroborated your hunch about Lucas and Pinkston. I'm only telling you this because you need to be doubly careful now. We want to wrap this operation up in the next couple of days, if possible."

"What about the car Johnny bought? Did you learn anything about that yet?" Katherine asked

"We found the car dealership that sold Johnny the car—a small sleazy lot in Miami. The date checks out, and it *was* a cash deal. The dealer cooperated after we gave him a hint of how much trouble he might bring upon himself if he didn't help us. Still, we don't have any really solid proof against Johnny. Big Buzzy is worth a pile of dough. He could say he gave the money to Johnny. About all we can prove against Johnny, right now, is that he used false identification papers."

"A good lawyer could get him off with a reprimand," Lee said, disgusted.

"We're still working on that, Lee. We do have Katherine's testimony, which is more than we had. And that leaves us with two things that still stump us. Our investigations indicate that there is some other biggie besides Lucas—maybe a boss, or maybe a partner to Lucas. You two would be amazed how much we've learned in the last two days."

"What's the other thing that eludes you?" Lee asked seriously.

"The cabin they mentioned. We hoped to find the rest of our answers there. It may contain the records and proofs we need. We've checked every property that has anything to do with Amano or Lucas. There's nothing you could call a cabin. We've checked leases. We've looked at shacks. We even checked out a houseboat Buzzy owns. No luck on any of it."

Rob looked at Katherine.

"We have someone checking out this Billy you told me about, and we're also trying to locate Johnny's car. It's parked somewhere, and that could give us another clue."

Katherine and Lee listened in silence.

"Now, Katherine, could you give me a detailed

account of your boat trips to Marco. Do you take one tomorrow?"

"Yes, at one o'clock. I usually take a sales associate and one to four prospects. We take the Intracoastal on the way there and come back by way of the Gulf. We dock at the condo dock, and I accompany the party while they look at the condo. After that, we take them to the restaurant I told you about—the place I saw Billy."

Rob looked at his notes.

"The Captain's Cabin Seafood Shack?"

"Yes...always there. We...that couldn't be the cabin—could it? I mean, they wouldn't use a restaurant, would they?"

Rob's expression didn't show the slightest hint of change, but he rose immediately and went to the next room to use his phone.

"What did you say your line of work was before real estate?" Lee asked.

"I should have thought of it sooner." She was pleased at his implied praise. "I've been there almost every day, have called it the Cabin many times, and I never associated it with the cabin we're trying to find."

Rob returned, this time wearing a broad smile.

"Almost there, I think. For your own protection, I don't want either of you to know what happens next, but we're probably only one or two days away from arrests. Katherine, whatever happens, we'll take you into protective custody until after the trial. Right now, you're our most important witness because of what you heard. Tomorrow will probably be your last normal day for a while."

"Normal? I've forgotten what normal means."

Rob chuckled and turned to Lee.

"We still haven't got a strong case against Johnny, unless something new turns up. But we'll get him for something, even if we can't convict him of murder."

Lee stared down at his clenched fists. Finally, he looked up at Rob. "Let's get him before he does more. In Chicago he almost added Kate to his victim list."

"He's a bad one. It's generally someone like Johnny who exposes these operations. Evidently, Big Daddy Buzzy has covered all his tracks thus far. Who knows what other crimes he's committed. We're sure that Lucas and the others know nothing about this incident with your aunt. Johnny Boy did that one on his own."

"Like the bank deal?" Katherine asked.

"Yes...but that was chicken feed...extremely foolish on his part. We probably never would have gotten to this point if it hadn't been for that."

"Your newspaper clipping, Kate. That's what got things rolling again," Lee admitted.

"I remember when I caught you reading it—you were, weren't you?"

"Of course. After seeing that picture I felt pretty sure you were mixed up in this."

"By the looks of your face, I think she's paid you back," Rob said drolly.

****

The next morning Katherine stopped to see Iris, knowing it would probably be her last chance for a while. Rob hadn't called yet, but she guessed he made a visit to the Captain's Cabin during the night. She hoped he found something.

"Make sure ya get back early, ya hear? It may

storm this afternoon," Iris cautioned with concern in her voice.

"If it gets bad while I'm there, I'll stay in Marco. I may get tied up in some other business, later. If you don't see me in church tonight, don't worry."

Katherine gazed out Iris's window. She couldn't tell her what was actually going on. She couldn't tell her that she might be somewhere far away by evening—waiting for an unpleasant trial where she would have to face people like Lloyd and Buzzy and Mr. Pinkston. And yes, she would probably have to face Johnny again, too. She shivered. Could she truly feel safe when this was over? How could they make certain they caught everyone? She tried to shake off her fears and remind herself that she was helping to stop terrible crimes. *That is enough. God, give me strength to see this through.*

She brought her attention back to Iris, ready to apologize for drifting off, but found Iris as far away as she had been. Iris stared at her seashell cupboard and seemed deep in thought—or memories. When they finally parted a short time later, Iris took her hand and squeezed it with more anxiety in her voice than usual.

"Be real careful, ya hear? Be careful out there. I'll pray for your safety."

Her trip to Marco went well, and Katherine arrived back at the boat slip ahead of the bad weather. In a couple of hours, she would meet Lee at a restaurant and receive an update on everything. Satisfied that she had plenty of time, she thoroughly cleaned her already clean boat. Tomorrow it might be in someone else's care for a while, and she didn't want to feel ashamed of her housekeeping.

When she finished that task to her satisfaction, she

gave her attention to fixing herself up for the meeting with Lee. She was all too aware that this might be the last time she ever went out with Lee. He might show no more interest in her when the arrests and trials culminated.

Time to go the limit.

She pulled out her favorite and most expensive dress, the one she had saved for something special. Now that time had come. The shimmering creation would have been the plainest of white sundresses, except for the exquisite cloth. It wasn't exactly white, but more opalescent. Its sheen seemed to come from the phosphorescence that shined out of the Gulf at night, and she had found high-heeled sandals that exactly matched.

She quickly stepped into the dress. With drop-earrings of single pearls, and another pearl in the hollow of her neck, she felt satisfied that the image in her mirror would pass the grade. The dress added a new dimension of green to her eyes while her hair flowed gently about her bare shoulders. And she was to meet him at a fast-food restaurant! She laughed at the absurdity. *I can't believe I've saved this outfit for a fast-food place.*

Lee waited at the restaurant door and looked exceptionally well—as if he might also have dressed especially for the occasion. He wore the gray suit she remembered from Chicago, and his hair blew out in the same way it did that day. His usually dark face looked pale and weary. When he saw her, his eyes flashed their approval. At length he shook his head as if to throw off a vision. "Let's go somewhere else. I can't take you to dinner here."

"This is fine—and safe. Let's hurry in. It's starting

to rain, and I'm blowing away."

"OK, but see if you can find a semiprivate table. By the way, what does a lady dressed like that eat in a place like this?"

"Whatever you order will do nicely."

They both kept their voices low while they ate.

"The Captain's Cabin was the place. They kept more information there than Rob had expected. Rob had a search warrant, but managed to get in and out without discovery, so no one there has a hint about what will take place shortly. The FBI will confiscate everything in the safe and make arrests at the same time. Our only orders are to act ordinary for a short while longer. When we leave here, we just wait."

"Lee, today on my boat trip I remembered something else that I never mentioned. I don't know if it means anything or not, but on a couple of trips to Marco it seemed that someone might have boarded my boat while I toured the condos. It even seemed like someone might have run it. I found water, and ashes, which had no reason for being there, and on two occasions my gas gauge read incorrectly. I saved the ashes in an envelope. They're in my cabin now. I had totally forgotten them while collecting all the other information."

"Do you remember which trips?"

"Yes. Both times Johnny came. The dates are in my logbook. The second trip was the day you followed me in the rain."

"Let's go back to your boat, and you can show me where you found the ashes."

By the time they arrived at the *Miss Iris*, a stiff wind almost knocked her over and the rain came down furiously.

"I found the ashes here around the hatch cover, and I smelled pipe or cigar smoke in the hold below. Nothing else looked amiss, and I've never noticed any odor of smoke since that day. Wait and I'll get you the ashes."

"Yes, go ahead. Rob will probably want them. I'm going to examine below for a minute." he kneeled to lift the cover.

"Lee, come here. Someone entered my cabin while I was gone. The pillows are—d-different. The covers aren't smooth and that drawer isn't closed tight."

"Your lock looked all right, didn't it? Does anyone else have a key?"

"Only me."

"Check and see if anything is missing. Take your time. Don't overlook anything."

Katherine looked in the drawer where she kept the envelope of ashes and found it there. She handed it to Lee and went through her other belongings. "It looks like everything is here, but I know for sure someone broke in because I cleaned everything perfectly before I met you for dinner."

"I'm supposed to meet Rob now. I don't think you should stay here."

He tried to reach Rob, but the line was busy.

"Lee, the intruder didn't find anything. I should be safe here. Go ahead, or you'll be late. Tonight's the night, isn't it?"

Lee looked embarrassed.

"Go on. I can reach you on your cell phone, can't I?"

"It'll be with me everywhere. I'll call you in a little while, and I'll be back when we're finished. Keep your door barred. Do you want a gun?"

"How about a two-by-four?"

He grinned.

"Goodbye." She shoved him out of the cabin.

It was dark and the storm had grown fierce. The rain lashed against the metal roof of the boat dock. She went over everything that had happened. She needed it clearly in her mind if she must recount it before a judge and possibly a jury. *I'll have to identify these criminals and testify against them. What an unpleasant job,* she thought as she pulled out the drawer where she kept the bank clipping.

She wanted to see Ray Pinkston's face again and imagine what it would be like to face him in court. Nervously she went through the drawer twice, but found no clipping. She had seen it only a few hours ago when she cleaned. She had taken the time to refold it and put it on the bottom of the other papers. It hadn't seemed important at the time, but now it was gone.

18

Goose bumps traveled up and down her spine as she dialed Lee's number. *Now someone knows that I know.* The thought kept blinking off and on in her mind like a caution light. *It must have been Johnny. He's the one who's been watching me, who tried to run over me. If he's seen that clipping, then....*

"Hello," came Lee's anxious voice.

"Lee, I found something missing."

"What?"

"The picture. The newspaper clipping with the bank picture."

There was silence for a second, and she waited tensely.

"Are you absolutely sure?" It was Rob's voice this time.

"Absolutely. I had it in my hands a few hours ago. I remember when I put it away. It's definitely gone."

"Listen to me carefully, Katherine. Go straight to your car and drive to some busy public place, or go to the police department. Keep your phone with you. Don't let your anxiety show and don't tell anyone anything. Sit tight and wait for my call. Go immediately, understand?"

"Y-yes, g-goodbye." Katherine tried to gulp down her fear.

With her cell phone in her small bag, she locked the cabin door. It was extremely dark outside. At first, she thought the storm had caused that intense darkness, but soon realized the light at her section of dock wasn't on. She looked at the spot where the light should have gleamed and could just make out the broken piece of glass cover that hung below it. It blew noisily back and forth as the violent gusts of wind had their way with it.

When she stepped lightly onto the dock beside her boat slip, she saw the shadowy outline of someone near her car—a man, a large man, big enough to be Johnny! She couldn't go back at that point because he obviously had a key to her cabin. There was no one around to help, and he stood between her and her car.

Rather than climb the short wooden stairway to the parking area, she turned down the main dock and walked as if nothing was unusual, as if she only intended to visit someone on another boat—except there was no one to visit. She studied possibilities. The slips ahead of her held a few medium sized boats followed by a larger one. On the other side of that large boat, a short section of dock ran at right angles to the main dock.

She felt the vibration as the man jumped down onto the wooden planks somewhere behind her. Her only chance lay in taking advantage of the darkness and storm. She quickened her steps until she passed the large boat, then ducked low and turned up the adjacent section of dock where, for a split second, the height of the boat hid her from his view. When that second arrived, she slid her purse strap over her head and lowered herself into the black oily water beside the boat.

Silently she worked her way to the bow of the boat where the water was rougher. She let her shoes drop off, and with only her head out of water, she moved on towards the next boat.

She couldn't see the man, but she heard his leap onto the large boat. Even the din of the storm didn't cover the loud thump of his landing. She instantly ducked under the closest section of dock, risked a hurried look, and ascertained it was Johnny. By his manner, she could tell that *this* Johnny had thrown aside all caution. The charade had ended. It had become an out and out chase.

She struggled to put distance between them and headed back in the direction of her own boat. When she reached the *Miss Iris*, she felt tempted by the slight security it offered, but quickly thought better of it. She reached her arm over its side, dropped her purse into an empty bait bucket, and moved out into deeper water.

From her new location, she watched Johnny run down the ramp beside the large boat. She had to fight off the panic that welled up inside. At least he hadn't located her yet, and now she was unencumbered by shoes or purse.

It seemed that her best opportunity for escape lay in crossing the narrow canal in front of her boat slip. With the rough water and heavily sheeting rain, she would be almost invisible as long as she stayed low in the water. A weedy piece of vacant land lay directly across the way. If she could reach it, she might be able to crawl across it to safety.

She struggled out to the midway mark where stronger current and choppier water pulled and tossed her about like a fleck of sea foam. With Johnny so close, she didn't dare swim naturally, but it was difficult to make much forward progress as she dog-paddled and treaded water. In due course, she reached the other side, but further down than she intended.

On hands and knees, she ascended the bank at a section of missing seawall. Flattened tightly against the ground, she started to slither across the field of wet sand and sandspurs. During the slow painful travel, her clothes and flesh picked up every available sandspur. When she lifted her head to look around, she saw another man not far ahead of her.

This man had a flashlight. He shined it on the water and the boat docks and obviously was working with Johnny. He cut off her escape route in that direction, but he hadn't seen her, yet.

The slashing rain was her salvation. On a clear night the scanty growth would never have hidden her. Katherine started the tedious slither back to the water's edge, not daring to look again. She held her breath as she crawled down the exposed bank and lowered herself into the black depths. The water greeted her like an old friend, and she was loath to leave it again. Almost totally submerged, she rested and pulled a few of the more painful sandspurs from her hands while contemplating her next move.

The other side of the canal looked safer because there were boats and docks she could use for cover, but Johnny was there. Still, she knew she would have to go back—and quickly—before that flashlight disclosed her whereabouts. The only other choice was the big open bay, and it looked rough and frightening. She would use that as a last resort. Only if it came down to a choice between the bay and Johnny, would she venture out there.

The trip back presented more difficulty than her first crossing. She ended up at the last landing before the bay itself. In the turbulent water there, she held onto the dock edge and pulled herself high enough to locate Johnny. He had moved closer to the other end and now had a flashlight. He would see her if she dared cross the big empty parking lot to its entrance.

For an instant, she considered making a dash for it. She had always been fleet of foot, though not impressively fast on short runs. She measured the distance and decided against such a gamble. With Johnny's long legs, he would quickly outdistance her, even if he was out of shape—and he wasn't.

Under the partial cover of the dock, she worked her way back in the direction of the *Miss Iris*, pulling herself around boat after boat. At times, her bare feet sank deep into the slushy silt, and more than once she cut them on sharp objects lying on the bottom—the garbage of thoughtless boaters.

When she neared the *Miss Iris* again, for a brief instant she considered taking it out. If she could get it to drift with the current, she wouldn't have to start the engine until she had floated out of hearing range. She still entailed great risk if one of them saw the boat leaving. Her plan wouldn't work unless she could manage a good head start. They would probably steal a boat and go after her as soon as they realized.

At that instant, a car pulled into the parking area, not far from where Johnny stood. She hoped for Lee or Rob, but only a lone boater a man she had seen a couple of times before, emerged from the car. He had come to check how his boat weathered the storm.

Please don't leave, she silently pleaded.

She resisted the temptation to call out and endanger him, as well as herself. He had left his car lights on and motor running. That meant he wouldn't be there long. Katharine watched him go down to his boat and begin to adjust the mooring lines.

It took her only a second to decide. She would take advantage of the interruption the only way she could. While still in the water, she quickly loosed the *Miss Iris's* mooring lines and eased the boat to the end of its slip. With a tight grip on the stern, she planted her feet against the end of the dock and gave a mighty shove. The *Miss Iris* glided into the canal soundlessly.

Katherine grabbed hold of the closest line and followed in the dark water behind it. If they saw the boat, they at least wouldn't see her, and she might still escape by committing herself to the sea. She helped the boat's progress all she could, but as soon as the current got hold of it, her efforts proved futile.

The *Miss Iris* developed a mind of her own and there was no stopping her. The wind and the current hurried her along, sometimes sideways, sometimes backwards, but straight on into the main channel of the bay.

Katherine floundered in the violence, was pushed under by low waves, and at times, flung roughly against the out-of-control boat, but all the while, she held tight to the line. Choking and sputtering, she tried to board the tossing vessel, but slipped back, swallowing great mouthfuls of sea. She tried again and entered, along with a deluge from a wave that broke against the boat just as she climbed over the slippery side. She slid against the wooden bait box and wrenched her arm. Pain shot through her, wrenching her insides, too, and she felt ill for a minute. At length, an overpowering sense of urgency brought her back to the immediate danger.

Visibility was poor, but she could still make out

the boat docks and could still see the lights of the boater's car. It looked like he was backing out. It would only be minutes before Johnny noticed the absence of the *Miss Iris*—if he hadn't already.

Chilled through and through, her hands shook too much for efficient work. She reclaimed her boat keys from the soggy purse that still lay in the bottom of the bucket, only now the bucket contained water. She had a flash of hope when she saw her cell phone, but its inner workings hadn't survived the lengthy bath.

The storm carried her along quickly and recklessly, but she couldn't risk starting the engine or turning on lights that close to the marina. She gripped the wheel and waited, praying the boat wouldn't capsize before she drifted out of sight and sound of her pursuers. Another wave hit her broadside, pouring in more of the deep. When she and the boat recovered from the shock of that, she studied her surroundings once more. Seeing only darkness, she turned the key.

The engine sputtered and coughed, reluctant to start.

Continued efforts left her greatly concerned that she would drain the battery before the engine cranked. Without warning, another wave sent her to her knees on the wet deck. She regained her feet, held on as best she could, and tried the ignition repeatedly. Finally, the chug of the engine became a steady sound in the fierce night.

She turned on both of the bilge pumps, and with a tight hold on the wheel, she headed into the waves. The waves weren't high, and now that she had control of the boat, she could keep more water from pouring in.

Without lights, she couldn't get her bearings, but

she knew she must be nearing the Gulf. She would have to turn the boat around. The *Miss Iris* might handle the conditions in the bay now that she had power, but the wild Gulf wouldn't act so obliging. Already the waves had grown higher and more menacing, and she was afraid the boat had already entered the Gulf waters.

Preparing to make a wide circle before the waves became too high for such a maneuver, she saw the dark outline of mangrove directly ahead of her. She had gotten out of the main channel and risked running aground, but at least she was still in the bay.

At once, she made a starboard turn and managed to pull away in time. It wasn't long until she sighted a buoy and knew she had returned to deep water. With it as a guide, she made her turn and headed back up the channel.

Now Katherine traveled towards Johnny, and had to keep careful watch ahead for pursuing boats. She scanned the port shoreline for a place to tie up. When she felt she had covered about half the distance she had traveled earlier, she eased closer to shore. The little inlet at Iris's house lay somewhere ahead, and she had to find a place to stop before reaching it. She couldn't risk getting that close to the marina and Johnny.

Before long, Katherine made out the dim lights of street lamps or houses along the shoreline and immediately set her course towards them. There was risk of running aground, but she had to take the chance. She saw an opening ahead of her. She cautiously entered it and discovered some pilings on one side as if a dock might have stood there once.

Cautiously she brought the *Miss Iris* in close and moored her as securely as possible. It wasn't as rough there, and the boat's fenders were still down from when she docked earlier that day. Satisfied that she had protected the boat as much as possible, she moved on to the business of protecting herself.

Katherine had to distance herself from the boat as quickly as possible. If someone traveled the bay in a boat, they might turn a light in that direction and certainly see it. The throbbing of one of her cut feet made her aware of the handicap bare feet might present if she had to run. She located her deck shoes and pulled them onto her abused feet.

The *Miss Iris* sat only ten feet offshore, but too far for Katharine to jump. She involuntarily shuddered and again lowered her tired, benumbed body into the rough water. Surprised at the depth, she swam the few feet to land.

The area looked unfamiliar, but she saw houses nearby and felt comforted. She turned right at the first street she came to and headed in the direction of where she hoped there might be businesses. Dogs barked constantly, giving away her whereabouts to any interested listener.

Impatient to leave that neighborhood, she saw a large vacant lot and cut across it at full run. A loud chorus of frogs and insects warned her just in time to save her another wetting. She had almost plunged into a pond. Covered with lily pads, it looked like a grassy field there in the dark. Three feet from its edge, she discovered her error and slid to a stop.

Though Katherine couldn't possibly be any wetter, she still felt thankful to be saved the shock of another dunking. Catching her breath, she looked down at her bedraggled dress. It had become home to a couple of hundred sandspurs. She detoured around the pond and passed by a rustic bench positioned near the water's edge. The bench jogged her memory. She had driven by that bench and pond before.

I'm not far from Iris's, but that also puts me close to Johnny and his friend...if they're still there. I can't put Iris at risk, but I might tap on her window and have her call the police. That shouldn't endanger her.

At Iris's house, the outside lights were on at both the front and back door. The bedrooms on her side of the house were unlit, but the windows were open. She crossed cautiously to the one that should be Iris's bedroom window and tapped gently at first, then a little louder when no one responded. When still no answer came, she put her mouth close to the screen.

"Iris," she called as softly as possible. She thought she heard someone stirring and a chair sliding out.

Captain Dale came to the window.

"Captain Dale, I'm in danger. I need you to call the police."

"Katherine, is that you?"

"Yes. Men are chasing me. I don't want to endanger you and Iris, but please call the police and have them come here. I'll hide somewhere until I see them arrive."

"Katherine, come inside. Iris hasn't come back from church, yet. No one will know you're here. Come in the back door. Come on. Hurry."

"OK, but turn off your light first."

When she saw the back yard darken, she hurried around to the door. He held it open, and she stepped into the house. In the unlit room, she could see him across from her. She tried again to make him realize the peril of her situation. "I can't hide here. This is too close to where I saw them last."

"Who? Why would someone come after you?"

"They fear what I know about them."

"What do you know about them?"

She hesitated only a second. "Enough to put them in jail. I have to go back outside now. Call the police and have them come here, please. I'll see them."

She reached for the door and something hard hit against her shoulder blade. An arm came around her neck.

"Turn on the light, Cap," Johnny said menacingly.

When a small lamp came on, Johnny jerked her around roughly and held a gun against her.

"Close that door." he rasped at Captain Dale.

The captain calmly shut the door and sat down on one of the kitchen chairs.

"Well—snoopy Katherine—where's your boat?" Johnny asked.

"I moved it," she choked out in shock.

"Set it adrift?"

"It's tied."

"Good. We'll find it." He directed his attention to Captain Dale. "We'll take her in your speedboat until we locate hers. She can go down with it. Shame to waste the boat, though."

"It's worth a heap more than you," Captain Dale said grimly. "But I reckon we don't have much choice left. Did your daddy tell you to go after her?"

"I can't find Dad."

"So you thought this up all by your lonesome?"

"Dad and Lucas gave me this job. I've been watching her to see if she was on to anything."

"And if she was, you were supposed to wait for orders, right?" He sat there calmly and never met Katherine's astonished eyes.

"What would you know about that?" Johnny asked hotly.

"Where'd you leave Lester?" He ignored Johnny's question.

"He's watching back at the dock, in case she wasn't on the boat."

"In other words, you decided to take over your daddy's job, and involve Lester and me in your mess."

"I told you I couldn't find Dad—and there wasn't time. You'd better be glad I acted fast. It's your neck too. Who are you, to be telling me my job, anyway? A lousy pickup man. You don't even know what's going on."

Captain Dale looked at him with menace in his eyes, but when he spoke, it was with the same easygoing drawl he always used. "I know you've gotten yourself into a tight spot. We'll have to go ahead now, but it'll be rough goin' out on the water tonight."

"If she can, then we can. Nobody will be surprised that something like this happened to a fool woman who went boating on a night like this."

"Get on down to the boat with her," Dale said gruffly and slid into his slicker.

Katherine's exhausted mind and body had received this final blow with no prior warning. She felt too tired, too stunned, to react to this new situation— but knew she must. The barrel of the gun hadn't left her body since Johnny first grabbed her. She couldn't risk anything while he held it tight against her, but she had to be ready. If that gun moved an inch...

Johnny impatiently grabbed her hair with the large paw that wasn't occupied with pressing the gun against her, and brutally propelled her across the long backyard.

"You run the boat. I'll hold her," he barked at Captain Dale when he neared the dock.

"Katherine, would ya come up here a minute. I have somethin' for ya," The trembly voice somehow sounded intensely clear in spite of it quiver.

Iris had drawn everyone's attention. She stood there in the back yard—witness to the whole, terrible scene. Her long, gray hair had come down and blew about her head. Her shining face looked beautiful in its moment of resolution.

"Get back to the house, Iris," Captain Dale commanded.

"Not until Katherine comes," she quavered stubbornly.

"Get in the house!" he shouted without his usual complacency.

"If I go in the house, I will call the police," she called out.

Thoroughly angered, Captain Dale started towards her, but was checked suddenly by the sound of a shot. He turned towards Johnny, who still pointed his discharged gun in Iris's direction. Captain Dale spun back and saw the crumpled form of his wife lying there in the wet grass. He jerked as if the bullet had entered his own body. He hesitated for a second, started across the yard towards Iris, abruptly changed his mind, and turned back to Johnny. "Y-you f-fool!" he stammered as he furiously approached. "You dirty, trouble makin'..."

Johnny shot him before he finished his sentence, but the bullet didn't stop his approach. He leaped at Johnny and knocked the gun to the ground. Johnny tried to hold on to Katherine and ward off the old man's fierce attack at the same time, but Captain Dale was beyond pain or caring. His impassioned assault proved more than Johnny could handle with only one hand, and he released Katherine's hair.

Katherine dove for the gun that had done such horrifying damage. She meant to put the weapon and herself as far from Johnny as possible. When she glanced behind for a brief instant, she saw Johnny bring his huge fist down on the captain's neck.

Captain Dale's limp body dropped beside her even as her hand made contact with the gun.

Before her fingers could close around the wet metal, something exploded in her head. For a second she dreamed that Johnny had stuck her head in an electric socket and stood there laughing at her...and then came blackness.

****

Consciousness returned slowly to Katherine. She could hear sounds, hear a motor, and feel the vibration of it against the back of her head. Water splashed on her from somewhere as she rocked back and forth.

She tried to move, but her body felt dead. Conscious enough to know she was lying on her back, she reached her hand around to explore her surroundings. Something lay close beside her. Her hand contacted a wet slicker.

Her eyesight cleared along with her memory. She was lying in the bottom of a small boat. Captain Dale was directly beside her, and she wondered if he was gone yet. She reached for and found his hand, which felt warmer than her hand. *Iris must be here, too.*

Katherine was too low in the boat to ascertain their location, but she guessed they were somewhere in the bay. Above, she could see the sky clearing. The last of the clouds were blowing away, and pale moonlight glimmered through, enough for her to make out Johnny at the stern, operating a large, outboard motor. From his constant backward glances, she could tell he worried about pursuit.

All at once, he turned and reached for something. What was it? She had barely closed her eyes before the flashlight beam searched her face. Its light glowed red through her closed lids. She held her breath until it grew dark again, then opened her eyes warily.

She must vacate the boat before Johnny reached his destination. That was imperative. The water's turbulence hadn't lessened, but she would gladly risk that now. If only she could take a quick look to see what land lay near—even a mangrove clump would do. She must steal over the side the next time he looked behind him. Silently she slid off her shoes in preparation, and silently she prayed, Lord, I need You beside me again. I'm as desperate as I was that morning in the garbage barrel, and I know I can't do this without Your help.

Johnny increased the boat's speed. He turned his attention totally towards the rear now, with only brief glances ahead. She wasn't sure, but thought she heard another motor. Johnny definitely acted like someone under pursuit.

While he looked away, she rose to a sitting position to see if a boat followed. A bright spotlight beam approached from behind. It came terrifically fast. She couldn't risk a jump now, or she might end up in the path of the new boat.

Johnny turned back in her direction.

She huddled against the hull of the boat in alarm,

but he didn't seem to notice her, or else he didn't care at that moment.

Only after he fired two shots at the closely approaching boat, did Katherine notice the gun in his hand. She rose to her knees and thrilled at the speed of the approaching boat. It must be Lee's boat!

Fear for Lee helped Katherine conquer her own fear. Without hesitation, she lowered her body over the side of the boat and held on tightly with both arms. The impact of the water on her legs felt as if it would pull her in two, but she clung desperately. The next time Johnny raised his gun to fire, she used all her weight as leverage to rock the boat. The stunt worked so well she almost capsized the boat.

Johnny fell sideways, but didn't lose his gun, and immediately righted himself. He never looked in her direction, and she realized he probably attributed his near upset to the rough seas. She also realized she must hang over the side as long as Johnny held that gun because he could shoot her.

When the other boat was almost upon him, Johnny cut his motor and tried to get off a shot. He was taking aim when the other boat plowed into him. The jolt almost caused Katherine to lose her grip. Recovering her hold, she saw Johnny again taking aim.

She jumped her weight into the air while pushing down on the side of the boat, but her right arm slipped and her chin came down hard against the edge. When she looked again, Lee had leapt onto their boat.

A frenzied fight ensued, and she climbed back aboard to give what aid she could.

Lee was a big man, but no match in size to Johnny. They punished each other terribly, and she began to fear the outcome. She seized an oar as a possible weapon, but couldn't find opportunity to help. It was difficult enough just to keep balance on the pitching boat.

They started drifting away from Lee's boat, so she scrambled to the bow to let down the anchor. She lost her footing when the boat shifted. When she regained her balance, Lee and Johnny were both in the water.

She rushed to the stern and grabbed Johnny's long flashlight to use as a weapon. It was heavier and easier to handle than the oar. She turned it on and could see instantly that Lee was more at home in the rough water than Johnny.

Johnny worked so strenuously to stay afloat that he couldn't put up much of a fight.

Lee pounded him in the face every time he surfaced.

Finally, Johnny didn't surface.

Only Lee was there, struggling towards the boat and her outstretched hand.

"Throw me a line," he gasped. He snatched the rope from the air as it sailed over him and tied it around Johnny, who had surfaced again. Lee dragged him and when he boarded the boat, he reeled Johnny in and tied him securely. Lee left him lying in the bottom of the boat and almost leapt at Katherine. He took the flashlight and turned it on her—searched her from head to foot before he pulled her close.

Katherine started to cry, but only for a brief instant did she lose control. Thoughts of Iris made her pull away. "He sh-shot Iris. Captain Dale too."

"Sit here for a minute." He lowered her to the seat. "I'll run us over to my boat."

It took him a minute to weigh anchor and cover the choppy distance to his boat. She hastily climbed aboard and held the two boats together while Lee gently carried Iris over. He never stopped to check Johnny, or the Captain.

Carefully he laid Iris down and examined her by the light of the flashlight.

Katherine couldn't help thinking she still looked beautiful. Her mouth had a look of satisfaction.

Lee finally looked up and gave a nod. "We need to get her to the hospital."

Katherine felt hope soar and sent a heartfelt prayer of thanks to God. She sat down and took Iris's hand. Cold and miserable, she was finally taking that promised boat ride with Iris.

19

The seas had calmed, but it was still precarious travel, especially with the other boat tied on behind.

When boat lights appeared ahead, Katherine started in apprehension. "Lee," she shouted, "another boat."

"Coast Guard."

Two Coast Guard boats pulled close beside them. Rob rode in the larger of the two, and Lee waved to him.

"I have two customers for you back there. I don't know their condition, or if they're even alive," he shouted to Rob.

Men boarded the towed speedboat and carried Johnny and Captain Dale aboard the larger Coast Guard boat. Lee carried Iris.

"We need an ambulance on shore for Iris. She's been shot."

Rob took her from Lee's arms.

"Kate and I are heading to my house," Lee shouted as he started to leave.

"Lee," Katherine called to him. "Lee, I left my boat tied along here somewhere. I don't want to leave it. I hope it hasn't sunk."

"It's all right. I stopped at it on my way here. The key was in it, wasn't it?"

"Yes, and my purse, too, it's on the deck...somewhere."

"Don't worry," Rob told her. "The Coast Guard will bring your boat in, and I'll get your purse."

"I'll be at the hospital—with Iris."

"We need you to stay with Lee at his place until we get there. I'll check on Iris and give you any updates. We'll meet you shortly."

Katherine could see the weariness in Lee as he climbed back aboard. His knees almost buckled under him. They'd both survived a dreadful night—a night they'd never forget.

He sat down beside her at the helm, and she remembered something the Coast Guard and Rob should know right away.

"Lee, Captain Dale was one of them."

He turned towards her. "I know. We found that out—too late to save you from this. It was a drug and money laundering operation."

"I heard Johnny call Captain Dale a pickup man. Did he bring in drugs with the *Miss Iris*?"

"Yes—until he sold it to you. He let you do it for him, then. The *Miss Iris* would make pickups out in the Gulf after a small plane dropped off the goods. I'll explain it to you when we get home."

Within minutes, they arrived at his house. He docked his boat, took Katherine's hand, and they both stumbled up to the house.

"We think we got all the main people and a few of the little guys. Lucas and Pinkston have been in custody since noon. Buzzy, too. Johnny didn't know anything about that. He worked on his own again."

"There was another man after me at the dock."

"Lester Dodd. They caught him. He talked right away, and that's why I showed up as quick as I did."

"Quick? You took forever!"

Lee closed his eyes for a second and shook his head as if to wipe out his thoughts. His voice broke when he spoke again. "I d-didn't think we'd find you alive. The blood at Dale's house, and then I f-found your boat."

"Johnny shot Iris and Captain Dale. He would have shot me, too, but Captain Dale knocked the gun from his hand. Johnny must have struck me on the head with something when I reached for the gun. When I woke up, I was lying in the bottom of the boat alongside Captain Dale. I planned to j-jump overboard until I saw your lights." She trembled violently

He took her in his arms and held her. They were still hugging, taking strength from each other when Lee's phone sounded.

When he released her, he smiled and looked down at her sandspur-infested dress. "I think I just hugged a porcupine." He spent only a couple of seconds on his call before he put the phone away. "That was Rob. He said that Iris was alive and conscious. The doctors are removing the bullet. Captain Dale is still alive too, though not expected to last long. Rob will come by here soon, but we have time for hot showers. You go first while I make coffee."

"I don't have any dry clothes."

"Use my bathrobe for now. It's hanging inside the door."

The hot water relieved her shivering, but she had experienced enough water for one night. It stung her many injuries, and she was glad to step out to a dry towel. Borrowing a hair dryer she found on a shelf, she made quick work of her hair before slipping into his soft green robe. She tied the belt around her waist and left on her pearl earrings and pendant. They made her feel more dressed. The full-length mirror told her the attire looked satisfactory, and Lee's eyes confirmed it as he passed her in the hall.

She paused in the kitchen to sort out her thoughts. *We haven't lost everything.*

The aroma of coffee asserted itself, and she forced her attention to more practical matters. They both needed something hot to eat. She searched the refrigerator and brought out everything that had possibilities. He had obviously bought some groceries, a few, anyway. She found eggs and a package of sliced ham. In the crisper tray, she found grapefruit and oranges, and on the door, she found numerous ice-cream toppings, including maraschino cherries. She left the toppings, but put the cherries on the counter with the other offerings.

Katherine quickly peeled and sectioned the grapefruit and oranges, removing the membrane. She cut up all of them and filled a large bowl with the prepared fruit. Stirring in sugar and some maraschino cherries, she filled two crystal stem glasses with the concoction and placed them and the remaining fruit in the refrigerator to stay cold.

Next, she cut the ham into small pieces and let it brown slightly while she prepared eggs for scrambling.

Lee finished showering in time to let Rob and another agent in the door. They looked like they had endured a rather miserable night, too.

So much for my candlelight dinner, she thought as she got out two more stem glasses for fruit and broke some more eggs.

When Lee came in to see what she was doing, she put him to work.

"We need service for four, please—plates, cups,

saucers, silverware, and four slices of bread in the toaster."

He grinned and set the places while Katherine finished her work.

Rob and the other agent, whom they introduced as Kenneth, came in and viewed the modest feast she and Lee had set out. Though hesitant at first to accept the hospitality, in the end Katherine had to cook more eggs and fix more toast, and Lee had to make another pot of coffee.

When they had cleared off everything except coffee cups, Kenneth took down Katherine's account of the evening.

"Will I have to hide away until the trial?" Katherine asked.

"Probably not for long," Rob replied.

"Did you catch everyone important? Wasn't there supposed to be someone else working with Lloyd Lucas—a boss, maybe?"

"Actually, Lloyd Lucas didn't exist. He's really Donald Townsend, Captain Dale Townsend's little brother."

Rob seemed pleased with the astonishment on their faces.

"When we left the hospital a while ago, the Captain wasn't gone yet. He's a tough old salt. When he found out Johnny still lived, he wanted to talk. We have his signed and witnessed statement on everything. That's why it took us so long to get here."

"Did Captain Dale work for his brother?" Katherine asked.

"Not exactly. Many years ago, he and his brother started moving drugs by boat. Later they added a small plane to the operation, which Donald flew until things suddenly got too hot for him. He ditched the plane at sea and everyone thought he'd perished with it. He resurfaced in Chicago as Lloyd Lucas, and the drug business continued in an even bigger way."

"So they were partners?" Lee asked.

"Of a sort, but Dale bossed everything. The strange thing is that no one realized Dale actually ran the entire operation—mostly from Miami. He let everyone believe he only picked up the drugs. He told us he did it that way so he could better keep an eye on the business. *Only* his brother knew about that arrangement. From the very beginning, Dale called all the shots and handled all the major deals. To his credit, he avoided the rough stuff. He was a careful man, and that's why they got away with it for so long."

"Lee told me I ran drugs. When?"

"You just took the boat to Marco. With the spare set of keys that Dale gave him, Billy made the drug pickup while you were gone. Billy kept the drugs at the restaurant until they were distributed."

Katherine looked accusingly at Lee.

"*You* thought I ran drugs for real."

"But I only thought it for a while," he explained lamely.

Rob saved him by continuing, "You started the ball rolling, Katherine, when you threatened the bank with publicity right when a big deal was going down. They couldn't risk any investigations right then, so you got a ticket to Florida, and Buzzy had to foot the bill for your friend's house. We thought we had everything tied up and tried to make all our arrests early this evening, but Johnny eluded us. When he broke into your boat cabin and saw that clipping, he didn't know we already had his daddy and Billy in custody. All he could think of was to get rid of you before you told on him. He must have been afraid you recognized him from when he tried to run over you in Chicago."

"That newspaper clipping caused all this grief," she sighed.

"Yes," Rob said, "but it also opened up the entire case. We've closed down a large drug and money laundering operation, and have probably apprehended more than one murderer."

"I can hardly believe that Captain Dale actually ran something like that." The thought enormously saddened her.

"He ran it for so long he didn't even care about the money. His deceiving appearance and modest lifestyle are what made it work," Rob said.

"We doubt he'll live till his court date," Kenneth added. "He may be gone now."

"I know you can charge Johnny with murder if Dale dies, but what about Johnny's involvement with my aunt?" Lee asked.

"Agents are questioning him and Lester right now. We learned that your aunt went to buy a condo, and only Johnny was there to wait on her. He convinced her of the necessity for haste, and *cash*, in order to forestall another contract coming from a different agency. Lester was the bogus security guard who accompanied her to the bank. Apparently she dropped off that card to you earlier that day."

Lee groaned. "She always kept stamped cards in her purse so she could send notes on the spur of the minute. I've received many of them through the years. I guess Lester delivered her to Johnny, right?"

"We should know more about that shortly. We did learn that Lester supplied all their false IDs. When

Buzzy discovered that Johnny had gotten into trouble again, he had Lester make up false credentials for him, and then he sent him up to Chicago to work at the bank where they laundered the drug money." Rob rose from his chair.

"Now, Katherine, we'd like you to come with us to Fort Myers and sign some statements. We plan to hide you away for a while—until we see how our case goes and make sure we have everyone.

"Not until I stop at the hospital. I can't go anywhere if Iris's life is in danger."

"We'll stop by the hospital on the way."

Katherine headed toward the door and suddenly stopped. "I haven't any clothes. And I left my shoes in that speedboat. I can't go out like this."

The men looked at her in surprise, as if they thought she wore some sort of dress and not a borrowed bathrobe. Lee rushed and brought her a pair of his sandals, much too large, but at least they were dry.

Katherine sighed and slid her feet into them. "Oh well. Let's go. I suppose people at the hospital will think I'm a patient when they see this robe."

Katherine rode with Lee while Rob and Kenneth followed in their car. When they reached the hospital, Rob rushed over to them.

"I just had a call from one of the agents questioning Lester. They drove to his house and found not only Johnny's expensive car but another valuable, locked in a windowless bathroom. This particular treasure appeared weak and undernourished, but full of spunk. She insisted they take her to see her nephew."

"N-not...not..." Lee looked at Rob pleadingly,

afraid he had misread Rob's grin.

"I believe she said her name was Molenda. She'd been locked in there for three months and subsisted on boxes of dry breakfast cereal that Lester threw in to her. The house is in a very remote location. No wonder we never found the car—or your aunt."

"Where is she?" Lee gasped.

Rob had barely glanced toward the hospital before Lee made a dash towards the entrance.

Katherine followed as quickly as the oversized shoes would allow. She arrived in time to see him hugging a small woman right inside the doors.

"Shouldn't you be in bed?" Lee asked when they finally separated.

"No one's going to put me away in a room. I know my rights. I've been locked in a tiny room for more than three months, and now I need some space around me. Let's sit down here, though. I admit my legs are wobbly." She smiled at a disapproving nurse who stood nearby with a wheelchair. Lee helped her to a seat in the waiting room, and Katherine, her eyes full of tears, sat down with them.

"We thought you'd been k-killed. We thought..." Lee couldn't say more but just stared at her with an unbelieving smile.

"We?" his aunt asked with a knowing look in Katherine's direction.

"I'm sorry. I was so glad to see you I forgot my manners. This is..."

"I'm glad to meet you, Katherine," Molenda interrupted and shook Katherine's hand warmly. "You see, I already know your name and all about you. I got tired of those men asking me questions, so I asked a few of my own. From what I hear, you could use a hospital bed tonight yourself."

"All I could use right now is some more good news. But surely you must need hospital care after all that time as a captive."

She reached over and patted Katherine's hand. "I'll probably give in and accept their hospitality later. I'm looking forward to making the acquaintance of a bed after sleeping on the floor for over three months, but right now, I'm too excited to sleep. I didn't expect to live but a few more days. They were ready to kill me. You see, my time was up...could you please get me a drink, Lee. I'm rather choked up."

"I'll bring you a drink. Please don't stand up again," the nurse advised and hurried away.

"What do you mean by your time was up?" Lee's face had grown tense.

"All I can say is the Good Lord stepped in and helped me. I was so anxious to buy that condo and surprise you that I forgot to use my brain. When I came out of the bank with my money, both Lester and Johnny waited for me. They put me in Lester's back seat and drove off. When Johnny asked for my money, I knew what was up. And I knew enough to cooperate and act stupid, too.

"That was a l-low moment for me. I did some fast figuring and fast praying. I apologized to God for my bad judgment and asked for a quick dose of wisdom. After I'd settled matters with Him, I searched my purse for some object of defense. I found three weapons: a pen, some postmarked cards to you, Lee, and a new post office box receipt." She sat there smugly as if that was the end of the story.

"We're listening, Aunt Molenda." Obviously, Lee knew her well. "How could you defend yourself with those three items?"

She smiled sweetly. She had her audience. "I realized that if my death was worth forty four thousand, then triple that amount might keep me alive. While my captors watched the road, I wrote a note to you. I told you that my Maine property would close in three months, and I'd receive a check at my new post office box for one hundred, thirty three thousand dollars. I mentioned that I would have to sign for it at the post office, but intended to give the money to you as soon as I could take it to the bank. At the bottom of the letter, I wrote my new address and told you to send my mail there from now on."

"You never told me you rented a post office box."

"That's because I rented it right after I mailed you that card about the condo. I decided I might need a place to receive mail while I was moving. I intended to send you another card with the address, but I never had a chance. Oh, here's my drink. Milk!" She smiled at the nurse. "Thank you so much for your trouble."

"The doctor wants you to build back up, and I thought you might be a little tired of water," The nurse explained.

"Water and dry breakfast cereal. Ugh! You don't know how good this milk looks."

"I'll leave your chair here if you promise to have someone help you into it when you're ready to go to your room." The nurse grinned understandingly and walked into a nearby office.

"So you let them find the letter you were writing." Lee continued impatiently.

"I just about shoved it in their faces, I was so scared. They had pulled into a lonesome spot by the water and turned off the motor. While they read my card and had a brief confab, I prayed the hardest I ever prayed. Ultimately, they drove to an old house in the woods and locked me in a bathroom. I tried to break the door or break a hole in the walls, but it wasn't built like today's houses. The wood laughed at my feeble attempts to bruise it."

"How did they intend to get that one hundred thirty three thousand when the check came?"

"They threatened to kill you if I didn't cooperate in everything. Their threats would have worked if I actually expected to receive a check in the mail."

"That was quick thinking to come up with a number like one hundred, thirty three thousand, Aunt Molenda. But you know that three times forty four would be thirty two.

"Of course I know. But I sold my property in Maine for one hundred thirty three, right before I came down here shopping for condos. The old house wasn't worth much, but a developer liked the hundred acres that went with it. I should get that money in the fall, but the buyer won't send me a check in the mail. That part of my story was a bit of a fib."

Lee looked his surprise. "Why did you write three months in the card?"

"For the life of me, I don't know why. I suppose I wanted to give you plenty of time to rescue me if the plan worked."

Two large tears rolled down Molenda's cheeks, and both Lee and Katherine rushed to hug her. "I'd say your p-prayers worked, Aunt Molenda," Lee said as he wiped his eyes. "But Kate did more rescuing than I did."

"I thank both of you. And now, I have more praying ahead of me—your friend, Iris." She smiled at

Katherine. "She was awake after they operated on her. My room is next door to hers, so I crept in to see her when no one was looking and spoke with her for a few minutes before she fell asleep. She's doing fine."

"Thank you for visiting her," Katherine said. "After we check on her, I have to go into protective custody. I may not get a chance to see her for a while."

"Don't worry about Iris. I'll keep an eye on her for you. She's already my friend." She reached out a hand for Lee's arm. "Now, if you could help me to the wheelchair, I believe I'm ready to sleep."

20

After a brief visit in Iris's room, Katherine accompanied Rob and Kenneth to the Fort Myers office. Katherine slept most of the way and needed aid to walk when they finally arrived.

"I'm sorry. We want you to go through everything one more time, Katherine," Rob apologized, as he introduced her to two other men who waited in the office.

The one more time lasted over three hours. Near dawn, they took her to a comfortable motel. Without noticing all the measures put into effect for her safety, she collapsed on the bed and slept blissfully for fifteen hours straight. That evening she awoke when they delivered a meal to her room, but she fell asleep before finishing it, and didn't wake again until the following morning.

Fully rested by then, Katherine wanted to get on with her life. She needed a new job, boat repairs, and a place to stay. The last hospital report said that Iris was healing without complications, but Katherine wanted to visit her. She fretted and paced the motel room. Someone had brought her suitcase while she slept. It contained all the items she had requested, but she looked at the clothes in disinterest. Nothing seemed quite right. She needed to go shopping before she saw Lee—if he ever came again.

The next morning she arose early, after suffering a

troubled night of dreams. She awoke and knew, beyond any doubt, how much Lee meant to her. But what did she mean to him? After everything they had gone through together, were they still only friends?

He had never said anything to indicate he might feel more than that. He had held her close during extreme circumstances, but any warm-natured person might have acted the same. There had been no word from him since that night. Did that mean it was over? Should she forget him?

She sat on the edge of her bed and let hope flow through her. She wouldn't give up without a fight. *I'll go out and buy a magnificent dress, and I'll...a* knock on the door interrupted her mental declarations. "Come in," she called.

Lee burst through the door bearing breakfast.

Shock petrified her for a few seconds as her recent thoughts reverberated through her mind. Here he was, and she had no time to prepare. Her second look affirmed there were platters—two of them. *Ah, he plans to eat with me!* Katherine felt the color rise in her face when she realized that she not only didn't have on a new, knockout dress, but she also still wore his robe. What would he think? Her intended boldness fled. The silence intimidated her, and she tried to think of something commonplace to talk about.

"Lee, I don't know if anyone's remembered about my boat. It needs pumped out every couple of days."

"I've looked after it. You should dry dock it and get it repaired and painted."

"You forget that I don't have a job now. I'll have to hoard my money until I'm employed again."

"You may not have to worry about that for a while. You should receive compensation for informing.

These were mostly federal offenses, and they covered much more territory than you realize. I think you can afford to have your boat done."

"Could they start work on it right away?"

"I'll see to it. Any special orders? Paint color? What will you name it?"

"It will remain the *Miss Iris*. Rob just called and told me about Captain Dale's death. He said the hospital would release Iris shortly. Will she be all right? There's no one to look after her while she's recovering."

"Sure there is. Iris and Aunt Molenda have become great friends, and my aunt plans to stay with her until Iris is totally recovered. That's funny, because they're both so different. Molenda is rather assertive, and Iris is so easygoing, but they're both strong women. When my aunt heard that Iris wanted to visit Dale, and that no one would let her because of her condition, Aunt Molenda insisted that a nurse roll Iris's cot in beside Dale's bed. Iris got to talk with him for quite a while before he passed away."

"That's wonderful. I'm glad the women like each other. But you said Molenda was independent and used to living by herself."

"She is—or was. She told me that after all those days tucked away in that tiny room, she rather liked the idea of a little company now. By the way, I have a gift for you—not from me. Iris sent it to you. She had me get it from her house."

Katherine took the wrapped package. The tag read, "To Captain Katherine—Love, Iris."

She opened it in wonderment and found a handsome new captain's cap, all white, black, and gold. Katherine bowed her head and let the tears flow—happy tears, joyous tears. Lee sat silently beside her. When she finally sat upright, Lee placed the hat on her head.

"I think Iris knew Dale was involved in crime," Katherine said. "That knowledge is what shamed her into leaving church those many years ago. She often looked sad, as if she hid a secret."

"A terrible secret. But her heroic deed that night made the headlines."

"I'm so glad. She came from a large family—seven children. I'm sure it will mean a great deal to all of them." Katherine looked at the neglected platters of food. "Is this breakfast you've brought us? We'd better eat before it gets cold." She forced down a bite of cold scrambled eggs. "Was your boat OK after its bump?" she asked in an attempt at small talk. Her campaign to win his affection had gone kaput.

"Yes."

"It took quite a jolt." She put down her fork and stared at the cold food.

"Uh-huh."

"Will you have to testify in court, too?" She picked the fork up again.

"Yes."

His one-word answers maddened her, and she wished he wouldn't look at her. It flustered her, and her cheeks felt hot again. She considered jabbing the fork into him, but instead dropped it back onto her tray, set her tray aside, and stared at the wall.

"Have you seen Rob recently," she tried.

"Today."

"I'll bet *he's* glad this is all over," she tried again in desperation.

"Yes."

Embarrassed tears tried to fill her eyes. If only he would stop looking at her.

"What did you want to talk about now?" he asked quietly. "Don't you have any more questions?"

Her head snapped up. He was teasing her—and at such a time! She saw laughter in his eyes through the blur of her tears.

His closeness impeded her vision as he seized her and kissed her with lips that burned her face and neck, with arms that held her as if he never wanted to let go.

It's the robe. I always did look good in green. Thank You, God.

Thank you for purchasing this Harbourlight title. For other inspirational stories, please visit our on-line bookstore at www.pelicanbookgroup.com.

For questions or more information, contact us at customer@pelicanbookgroup.com.

Harbourlight Books
The Beacon in Christian Fiction™
an imprint of Pelican Ventures Book Group
www.pelicanbookgroup.com

May God's glory shine through
this inspirational work of fiction.

AMDG

medicam pultpops
stoma pouches
Cauesenes
sticks
tissues & wipes

1 h

CPSIA information can be obtained at www.ICGtesting.com
Printed in the USA
BVOW03s1158130614

356317BV00003B/83/P